Praise for Juan Eslava Galán's
The Mule

"I have enjoyed it like a compulsive reader,
from the first to the last line."
—Arturo Pérez-Reverte, author of
The Seville Communion

"An excellent, lighthearted piece of literature."
—*El Periódico*

"A novel of intrigue and espionage that
cleverly combines history with fiction."
—ABC Cultural

THE MULE

A Bantam Book / March 2008

Published by
Bantam Dell
A Division of Random House, Inc.
New York, New York

This is a work of fiction. Names, characters, places, and incidents either are the
product of the author's imagination or are used fictitiously. Any resemblance to
actual persons, living or dead, events, or locales is entirely coincidental.

Library of Congress Cataloging-in-Publication Data
Eslava Galán, Juan
[Mula. English]
The mule / Juan Eslava Galán ; translated by Lisa Dillman.
p. cm.
ISBN 978-0-553-38508-3 (trade pbk.)
1. Spain—History—Civil War, 1936–1939—Fiction. I. Dillman, Lisa.
II. Title.
PQ6655.S55M8513 2007
863'.64—dc22
2007036279

Printed in the United States of America
Published simultaneously in Canada

www.bantamdell.com

BVG   10 9 8 7 6 5 4 3 2 1

The Mule

Juan Eslava Galán

Translated by Lisa Dillman

BANTAM BOOKS

A mi padre, herrador y acemilero en la Guerra Civil

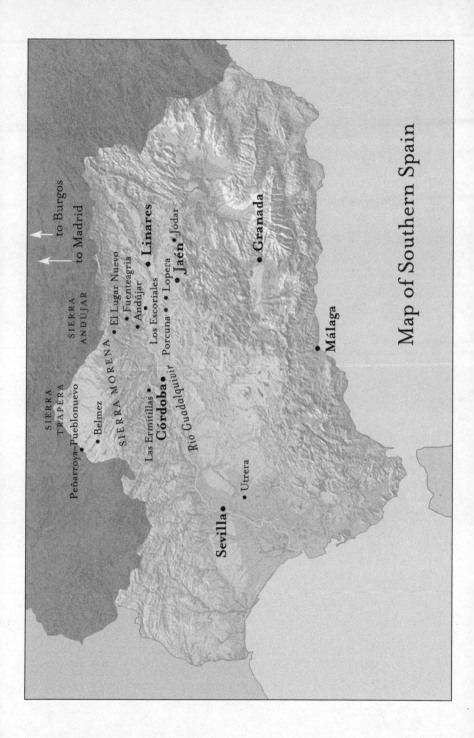

Map of Southern Spain

The Mule

Chapter 1

Juan Castro Pérez, corporal muleteer of the Third Battalion of the Canaries Falange, third company, is hunting for wild asparagus in the brush. Day has been attempting to break for some time now, but a dense, damp fog coils around the tops of the dwarf oaks and cork oaks, holding it at bay. Dewdrops trickle off the branches, burrowing tiny funnels into the sandy ground and rolling down the soldier's forage cap. Castro climbs a stony hill dotted with oaks and low scrub. A few granite crags jut out, halfway up. He's heading toward them when suddenly he stops and crouches, one knee to the ground, holding his breath, his heart pounding. Something moved in the fog, a gray shadow behind a patch of bramble.

Through his sidepack, Castro fingers the handle of the pistol Sergeant Otero lends him when he goes asparagus hunting. Getting caught by the reds is the last thing he needs. It's been a year since Castro switched sides, and if a turncoat falls prisoner, not even Jesus Christ Himself can save him from the firing squad. Deserter *and* traitor. It would mean court-martial, death sentence, ten shots, and into the ditch within a heartbeat.

Castro narrows his eyes and breathes deeply. He feels tiny droplets of icy water in his lungs. For a few interminable minutes, he awaits the enemy's next move. "Why send me out to hunt asparagus, when it's so nice playing cards back in the hut?"

The fog lifts a little. Shapes and colors slowly become distinguishable in the undergrowth. Castro makes out the familiar silhouette of a mule. Alone, or not? He glances around cautiously and cocks his ear, listening: just the unremarkable sounds of a country morning. That's all. He cocks the gun, and the *click-clack* of its well-oiled parts seems to embolden him. He crouches low toward the undergrowth, keeping his eyes peeled, alert. He circles the crags, walking around the sunny side, and sees the mule standing there, frozen, expectant, having sensed his presence. Castro surveys the terrain: the ruins of a cottage with a collapsed arbor, stone porch, the remains of some abandoned fig trees, a hayrick, rotting straw. No one. Maybe the mule got lost on the hill. She's not hobbled and wears no halter.

He approaches the animal. The mule cocks her ears nervously and starts, her eyes frightened. She raises her muzzle to reveal big, yellow teeth.

Castro knows animals. He's in charge of the regimental mule train. He speaks softly to the mule, who responds to the friendly tone of his voice.

"Hey, there! Shhhhhh. There now, pretty girl. What are you doing here, eh? Where's your master? Hey now, girl."

The mule seems reluctant, but when the corporal strokes her neck, she stretches her black muzzle forward to sniff him.

"Well, well, well. What are you doing here, eh? There, there. Don't be scared, pretty girl." Castro leans in so she can smell his body, places his open hands before her snout, and the animal's hot breath warms him. "What are you doing here, baby girl?" he whispers. "You lost? No master?" The mule flicks her ears, lets herself be stroked, feels the man's friendly hands on her powerful chest, on her loins, her ribs, which stick out a little. "Not too well fed, eh?" the soothing voice inquires.

The corporal's fingers slide gently to her hocks. The animal remains calm. She's well trained.

"A good, tame mule, eh?" he whispers approvingly.

Castro inspects his find with expert eyes. A fine-limbed mule, solid knees, shrunken belly, straight, slightly arched back. A good mule, the kind his father used to buy at the Andújar fair, this one an unusual ashy white. An excellent mule. He gazes into her lively, round eyes, shiny and hard.

"Where's your master, baby girl?" he whispers. "You with the army? The fascists or the reds? You lost?"

He crouches to examine her cannon bones, to see if there are scratches, any indication that she might have broken her hobble and run away. No sign of that. Castro studies her small hooves with satisfaction, notes that her horseshoes are new. The clinched nails show through the center of her hooves, two centimeters from the ground; she's well shod. Like a marquis—well, a marquise.

"What do you say, baby girl? You come over to the other side too? Which column are you with?"

The mule lets him stroke her strong jaw, her hard bony face, her downy-soft black snout, sprouting a few bristly patches of gray. But she doesn't respond to his question.

Castro imagines his arrival back at the company, his encounter with Captain Montero, announcing his find by the trenches. One more beast of burden he'll add to those already in his care, the twenty-four that make up the mule train of the Third Battalion of the Canaries Falange.

Castro takes the bandolier off his sidepack and ties a couple of knots, improvising a headstall. He transforms his belt into a makeshift halter.

"Not bad!" he says to the mule proudly. "No asparagus today, but this will do for now. Let's go."

On the slow walk back to the nationalist lines, he's pensive. He thinks about his poor family, the farmland they work for don Federico in La Quintería. Castro will never be a landowner, but a mule would be an undeniable asset.

The decision is simple. "I'll bring you to my father. We sure could put you to work back home when the war's over."

He looks at her and muses, "We don't know your name, now, do we?"

After a few more steps, he stops. The mule does likewise. Certainly well trained.

"Not going to tell me your name, eh? I'm going to call you Valentina, for being so valiant, placing yourself between the reds and the fascists, with all the shooting. Suitable: Valentina."

The mule pricks up her ears.

"You like that, eh? It's settled, then. Valentina."

He pats her neck.

Castro, leading the mule, takes a detour, returning the back way to the abandoned *cortijo* where the regiment has its stables.

A short, dark, stocky soldier steps forth. Less than a centimeter of forehead separates his single, long bushy eyebrow from a patch of bristly black hair.

"Where you going, Juanito? Where'd you get that mule?"

"She's on loan from the other battalion; they sent her to be treated. She's got a sore on her withers. Her name's Valentina." He looks at the mule and says, "Valentina, this is Chato. He's from Andújar too. Like me. A little slow, but not a bad person."

Chato shrugs.

"Okay."

That night, Castro fills out the train's regimental incident report. *Mules: 24; Horses: 5; Incidents: none.*

He doesn't count Valentina. He's decided to try to slip her through, unnoticed, and take her home when the war is over.

Chapter 2

June 19, 1938. Third Triumphal Year. The facade of the Prior *cortijo* has been hit by a cannon, snapping a palm tree in half. The kitchen of the *cortijo* is spacious, and its huge black sooty fireplace contrasts starkly with the whitewashed walls covered in graffiti and pro-Falange slogans: *Viva the Third Battalion of Regulars! Viva the Falange! ¡Arriba España! Antonio Pérez Latorre, First Company, Second Platoon, Soria Regiment, slept here, November 19, 1936.*

The cannon blast left a gaping hole in the wall that opens onto the stables, and although they've covered it with waterproof canvas, gusts of damp wind push through. The roof tiles have been removed and used to build shelters in the trenches. A summer storm, which has been pounding down all night, soaked the flat roofs so much that it's raining more inside than out. Castro balances an empty tin can on his lap, catching the monotonous, rhythmic drips of a leak.

As always, when the weather changes, the parasites become more active. The muleteers scratch their heads, armpits, and chests vigorously. Now and then, one of them will catch a louse and crush it or flick it into the fire.

Heliodoro is spit-roasting a strip of bacon on a piece of barbed wire. The fire flares up with the fat drippings. He takes it off, squeezes it between two pieces of bread, and bites down with gusto.

Aguado contemplates his comrades. Faces toasted from the sun, weathered by the elements and by work.

"We look like pirates," he says. "We look like the bad guys, not the handsome soldiers in new uniforms you see in the movies."

"Go on, say it!" Pino replies. "What we look like is a bunch of militiamen. If we walked into a convent looking like this, the nuns would faint!"

"That's what you're hoping for, isn't it? A convent full of novices . . ." Lieutenant Vico exclaims.

"It was just an example, Lieutenant. I've never been in one of those places, but I bet it smells good."

"Probably like incense," Aguado adds.

"And roses, from the cloister," Amor interjects.

"No," says Pino. "I meant like the smell at the dress-maker's."

"Starch?" Aguado asks. He was once a traveling fabric salesman and never misses a chance to flaunt his knowledge.

"Christ, no, you fool!" Pino explodes, bursting out laughing. "The smell of cunt when there's a bunch of women in the same place!"

"You think *nuns* smell like cunt?" the lieutenant inquires. "Idiot."

"Lieutenant, sir, kindly tell me whether nuns are women or not."

"Get out of here. Take your nonsense with you."

That's as far as they've gotten when the blanket-cum-door opens and a liaison walks in.

"Lieutenant, sir! Commander Soler's orders, sir: The mules are to head out; there's work to do."

It's the order they've been awaiting.

"All of them?"

"All of them."

Then, to his muleteers: "Let's go, then. No more sitting around."

There's still an hour before dawn. Lieutenant Vico finishes his cigarette and continues his rounds. The mule drivers tie on their tabards and head out into the night, into the cold, crisp mountain air.

"Let's see what today brings," Pino says, stretching until his bones crack.

They've been ordered to carry machine-gun ammo, mortar shells, and hand grenades. Which means things are really about to heat up.

In the hazy dawn light, the mule train climbs a steep, rocky path winding through the foothills of the Sierra Trapera. Each driver leads one mule by the halter, with two more tied behind, single file. Their hooves ring out on the pebbles. Flowering rockrose and rosemary line the narrow path, offering a bucolic contrast to the war. Castro thinks about the beehives he left behind in the Sierra Andújar, in El Lugar Nuevo. He's been gone for nearly two years now. Who's going to neuter the animals while he's away? His mouth waters, dreaming about eating bowls of honey swimming in oil, stabbing a crust of stale bread with his jackknife and drenching it, like bread soup.

Suddenly a distant crash as sharp as thunder rouses him from his fantasy.

"That'll be old Red, starting the dawn chorus," Cárdenas notes.

The mule drivers instinctively stop and strain to listen through the chirping flocks of birds. A few seconds later, the howling of mortar fire grows louder. The birds fall silent.

"Captain Atilano, that *cabrón,* telling us to rise and shine," the liaison says calmly, referring to the mythical communist captain they often blamed for attacks. "He must've gotten an early start this morning."

Two explosions rumble on the other side of the mountain. The ground beneath them trembles slightly. The animals prick up their ears. They've been through this before, though they'll never get used to it.

"Let's go, boys!" Castro orders his men. "Move it, let's get going, no sense hanging around here."

More shells whiz through the sky. Another half dozen explosions blast out on the other side of the mountain. Then the barrage stops and silence settles in once more. Birds sing again. Castro finally breathes easy. Same old story. Calm now, until next time.

The corporal doesn't know that the Tenth Division has just arrived from Madrid to reinforce republican positions and is preparing to launch a counterattack to retake Antigua and Cansino, on the flank of Peñarroya.

The convoy traverses a low plain dotted with oaks and wild olive trees. The mules and drivers cross a dusty riverbed and take up the path again; tractor prints and tank tracks are embedded into the ground. They reach the command post, housed in a dilapidated barn surrounded by a couple of sheds, all camouflaged with netting. Castro is updating a lieutenant when a sergeant blows the whistle. Air raid. Three small fighter planes have flown into view from the other side of the hill. They're flying low, against the rising sun, heading toward the trenches.

"Move!" Castro shouts. "Get the mules under the trees, now! Take cover!"

They get the animals out of sight just in time, as the fighters turn wide to make a second pass back toward

Castro and the muleteers. Tracers whiz furiously through the air, sending dirt flying. Soldiers who had just been picking off lice, chatting, writing letters, thinking about their far-off homes, dive into ditches. Three animals, standing half-unpacked, are left, forsaken, out in the open.

Castro, livid, emerges from his shelter behind a wall.

"Where the fuck are you, *cabrones*?" he shouts at his men. He finds them huddled behind the farmhouse wall. "Can't you see they're going to bomb the house, you fucking cowards? Get the mules under the trees—and stagger them! Heliodoro, over to that hill; Petardo, get back into the pines; Cárdenas, behind those rocks!"

While shouting orders, he runs to the three mules and takes them to shelter in a corral.

After a few passes, one of the planes changes course and heads for the command post.

"Watch out!" someone screams.

Castro hurls himself to the ground beside a granite wall and covers his head with his hands. One of the muleteers, Amor, hiding behind a big oak tree, realizes a bullet has hit the trunk, inches from his head. Before the planes return, he runs for the protection of the granite wall.

"Get down, here it comes!" Chato cries.

By the time Amor takes shelter behind a rock, halfway to the wall, the fighter has already machine-gunned the plain, creating two long furrows of flying earth and stones. The plane straightens course and turns to gain height. Amor feels something wet on his chest.

"My cognac!" he cries, devastated. "Lord, please let it be blood."

"You hit?" Castro asks, alarmed.

"Worse," the muleteer laments, feeling his chest. "They got my bottle."

He licks the liquor off his fingers.

The three planes fly off.

The muleteers drive their teams up the rolling hill single file, winding through scrub and oaks. On the other side, stray bullets whistle through the air; some pierce leaves or sever branches that fall like light rain on the convoy. The direct hits puncture tree trunks with dull cracks. From the crest of the hill, the battlefield emerges amid a thick, dusty cloud that tinges the land a weak brownish-gray.

Stretcher bearers run, crouching over, to retrieve the wounded. One hurries past Castro. Beneath a soiled, bloody blanket, he can see what remains of a thigh: torn, burned, carved flesh, white splintered bone contrasting the blood-red rags.

A mortar shell explodes fifty feet away. The mules, spooked, kick the air, freeing themselves of their loads. Castro is unaware of when he abandoned his. He's shaking, his face to the ground, feeling the explosions, not realizing that the gravel is scratching his cheeks. He wishes he could burrow underground like a worm or an ant, vanish into some deep tunnel where death can't strike.

Someone cries out. "*Madre, madre,* we're going to die!"

Castro recalls the day he first got to the Peñarroya

front. The mythical Captain Atilano had outdone himself. First a cannon blast, a long shot, then a short one—to correct—then a dozen shells fired over the hill at the convoy; they killed four mules and wounded five more, three of which had to be put down.

When he's able to regain his composure, Castro gets up to look for his men. Capitana, the best mule of the lot, lies kicking in a pool of blood and feces, hooves entangled in her own spilled guts, mouth foaming and full of dirt. Castro's eyes burn with tears.

"You, give me your piece," he orders a soldier.

The soldier hesitates but hands him his rifle. Castro pulls back the action. The bullet makes a sinister, metallic sound as it locks into the chamber. He walks over to a few feet from the mule, raises the rifle, takes aim, and fires at the animal's head. The mule exhales huskily, stops kicking, and slowly, almost sweetly, places her huge head on the ground.

Castro hands back the rifle.

"Fuck the war. What did these poor animals ever do to anybody?"

Aguado approaches him, having recovered his usual absent expression.

"How'd we make out?" Castro asks.

"Men, fine. Cárdenas took a shot in the thigh, but it's not bad. They're treating him now. The animals fared worse."

"Then let's unload and get it over with."

The muleteers finish unpacking and lead their mules to the shelter of the gypsum kiln. There's a moment of calm, mid-morning, as the respective armies regroup. The stretcher bearers use the time to evacuate the wounded. Men afflicted by superficial wounds hobble along on their own, at the rear, to the first-aid post, some leaning on those who can still walk properly. The worst are carried on the mules' handbarrows. Castro and his men make a few trips to the aid station.

They're given a cold meal: a crust of bread and can of sardines per head, and one can of Portuguese fruit in syrup for every four. They also dole out bottles of Avance cognac.

"Rotgut: good," Pino says, taking a swig.

"Bad," Aguado responds thoughtfully. "They're going to want us to use our *cojones* to take back that first trench."

They pass the bottle in silence. The cognac—pure alcohol with some coloring—burns their throats, muddles their brains, dissipates their fears, gives them the courage or recklessness needed to launch an attack to take back the trench they lost. The soldiers stare at one another, feigning indifference. How many of them will be alive tonight?

The cease-fire lasts barely an hour before it all starts up again: mortar fire, machine-gun spray, rifle shots. They've requested assistance from the air force. A flight of Heinkel 51 fighters makes a pass over the battlefield. The nationalists cheer wildly at the sight of the black circles beneath the wings, the crosses on the tails.

"It's our guys!" Pino cries. "Yeah! Fuck 'em good!"

The fighters circle slowly, diving in formation and machine-gunning enemy positions. Panic spreads on the enemy's side. Some throw down their arms and surrender, ignoring their commanders' threats.

"They're giving up! *¡Viva España!*" cries one soldier.

The sergeant glares at him, irate. "Shut your mouth, it ain't over yet!"

The republicans give up the trench they'd taken from the nationalists. Pounded by the air force, they abandon the positions they'd conquered and retire to their lines.

The two sides exchange a few more cannon blasts. Then all grows still again and, before nightfall, both sides come out to collect their dead. Castro and his men take them to the threshing floor at the Cadenas farm. From there, a truck will transport them to Peñarroya cemetery.

The medics see to the emergencies in an improvised shed, on an open packsaddle covered with an oilskin, the only one.

"Let's go! These four, get them to Valsequillo, to the field-dressing station."

"The trucks can't get here, Lieutenant, sir. The ambulances are in Rubia."

"Well, then, load them onto the mules."

"Yes, sir!"

"Muleteers, let's go!"

Castro approaches with six mules hauling makeshift stretchers. The stretcher bearers load up the wounded. One exhausted, baby-faced soldier wears a card on the button of his army jacket that reads: *Open wound. Approximation and suture. Drain,* followed by the doctor's illegible signature. A sergeant from Coria whom Castro recognizes from the mess hall wears a turban of stark white bandages contrasting with his dark skin, lending him an Arab appearance. His eyes are clenched and he's breathing laboriously. The diagnosis on his chest reads: *Skull. Rest, plug, wash edges.*

An unexploded mortar shell is lodged below the shoulder of another man carried on a stretcher. It bulges out of his chest like a breast, between two ribs. His clavicle is jutting out. The man is trembling, weeping, an expression of sheer terror defining his face, his eyes closed.

"That guy's in trouble," Chato observes.

"No," Heliodoro replies. "Not him. The doctors treating him are the ones in trouble. What if that baby blows while they're removing it?"

"What about us?" Aguado complains. "Who the fuck is taking him down to the first-aid post? I've had enough for one day."

They fall silent and glance over at Corporal Castro. It's his call.

"I'll do it," Castro says, his voice thick.

He looks down on the pretext of stomping out the cigarette he's just thrown on the ground, half smoked.

The wounded man is dazed from morphine, yet whimpering. Castro, leading the mule by the very end of the rope, as far as possible from the shell, chooses the path with the fewest stones and hurries to get out of this mess. The soldier moans and asks for water.

"Hold on, man, we're almost there. Let the doctors see you first. You might not be allowed to drink."

The soldier, after insisting incoherently, finally falls silent on the last stretch. Now and then Castro turns back and tries to raise his spirits. "Just about there, man. Not far now." The medics pronounce him dead on arrival.

They carry him gently to the back patio and set him down behind a stone basin by the well.

"Call the explosives experts."

Castro leaves, in no rush. Outside, he takes in a breath of fresh air, free of the stench of death, blood, and disinfectant.

All that danger for nothing.

Chapter 3

September 1, 1938. Third Triumphal Year. In the shed of an abandoned *cortijo*, the muleteers are sitting around a fire, eating a stew comprised of potatoes, rice, and donkey meat. A weak autumnal sun dissipates the morning's heavy rain clouds. After wolfing down his share, Chato wipes his aluminum plate with a handful of straw and locks it back into place beneath his canteen. He takes out a tin box full of cigarette butts, brushes away the old ash, then crumbles the remaining tobacco to roll a cigarette. He leans back on a packsaddle. After the first drag, he sighs.

"This is the life. Just sitting around scratching your balls, doing nothing..."

"You should be ashamed of yourself," Aguado reprimands. "Idleness is the mother of all vice. Just ask the *padre*."

"The mother of all vice?"

"That's what I said."

"Well, mothers deserve respect."

Corporal Castro appears, holding a sheet of paper, beaming.

"Attention, company! Listen up, you babies! I've got permission here for some of you to go change your clothes and get laid." He pretends to don a pair of imaginary glasses and prepares to read the names. "Wait. What's it say here? I can't quite make it out."

"Come on, Castro, just tell us. Don't keep us hanging!" Heliodoro protests.

"Ramón Aguado."

"What's Aguado going for? He don't even like to screw," Pino quips.

Aguado shoots him daggers. "Shut your mouth, limp dick. All you do is talk."

"Juan Cotrufes Pino."

Pino laughs, displaying his crooked teeth.

"And yours truly," Castro concludes. "That's it. While I'm gone, Chato's in charge of the mules, got it?"

Chato, who's finishing off what's left of his cigarette, raises a pot of greasy stew in acknowledgment.

The artillery truck is parked beside the barracks, its

hood open and folded up. The soldiers on leave load it with boxes of shells and settle themselves into the remaining space.

"Let's get a move on! Today!" complains the driver, a redhead wearing mechanic's overalls under a greasy fur-lined coat. "That everyone? Let's go, then, Linicio!"

The mechanic closes the hood and turns the crank vigorously. The engine sputters and coughs asthmatically to life. Linicio removes the crank and hops in, closing the door behind him.

"We're off."

Leaving a trail of thick black smoke behind, the truck drives through a countryside dotted with kermes oaks and scrubland, green fields and streams swollen by the rain. Cold, crisp air filters into the truck bed through the rips in the canvas roof. One of the soldiers has hung a pair of underpants from the roll bars.

"Who the fuck do those belong to?" Sergeant Barrionuevo protests.

"Me, Sergeant," one of the soldiers replies. "I washed them last night and they haven't dried yet."

"Well, you didn't do a very good job, because they smell like shit."

The others laugh. Their first leave, after two exhausting months of fatigue duty, has them in high spirits.

Castro thinks of Valentina. She'll be well taken care of in his absence; he told Chato exactly what to do. And at night, when Chato fills out the report, he'll list twenty-four mules, just like always. Valentina won't be counted. She's still on loan from another battalion.

The trucks reach Peñarroya and drive through town, taking the mine road, passing by some factories with a tall, smoking brick chimney on one end.

"They smelt pyrite here," one of the local soldiers says. "Mine silver and lead as well. The silver goes to France and the lead stays in Spain, for bullets."

"And what do the French do with the silver?"

"How the hell should I know? Probably make bracelets for their mistresses."

They cross the iron bridge over the Hontanilla stream and make their way into Pueblonuevo, driving down a few deserted streets, doors and windows closed, some even nailed shut. Blades of grass peek through the cracks in the pavement. Military personnel roam the streets. The evacuated civilians have waited two years for the front to move so they can return, though a few have come back to farm the land or make a living off the miners and soldiers.

Plaza Santa Bárbara has two taverns and a grocery store, plus a cheap canteen and two hostels. The Spanish and Falange flags fly above the town hall. The old social club next door has been converted into an aid station. On the frosted glass above the door, Castro reads, *Pueblonuevo Club del Terrible.*

The trucks pull up across from the old mining company store, where the Twenty-second Division has set up their command. The battalion's dented tin coat of arms adorns the main balcony below their flag.

The soldiers loosen the truck's back flap and jump out.

"Fall in!" Sergeant Barrionuevo thunders.

They do so, at ease. The sergeant counts heads and then warns them, "You have twenty-four hours to mess around. But tomorrow at eight o'clock sharp, you better be back here. If you get locked up, I'll tear into you so bad you'll remember it for the rest of your life. Got it? Okay, then. Fall out!"

Two rookies toss their caps into the air and begin cheering; the veterans fall out in silence. There's not a lot to do in a deserted mining town during wartime.

Castro, Aguado, and Pino wander the streets and plaza for a while. They down a few glasses of wine and chew peanuts in a miner's cantina. Pino, who can play a little guitar, asks the bartender for one of the instruments hanging on the wall beneath a filthy, fly-ridden sign that reads, *No singing.*

With practiced poise and a look of concentration on his face, cigarette dangling between his lips, eyes half closed, Pino strums lightly, tunes a few pegs, and tries again: It sounds worse than before. Aguado rests a hand on his shoulder and breaks into song, with more feeling than skill:

And beneath a tree with no fruit
I stopped and had a thought
A man with nothing to give

How few friends he's got
Beneath a tree with no fruit
I stopped and had a thought

Castro and the few patrons clap.

"Not bad, that soldier," says one approvingly. "Sings like a bird."

"A regular canary in a coal mine," Castro replies with a bright smile.

Two wheat-and-seed brokers, made wealthy by the army's patronage, buy them a round of drinks.

By the time they leave the bar, slightly tipsy, it's getting dark. A skeletal woman in a flowery apron and thick socks stands in the doorway of the Santa Bárbara chapel, selling roasted potatoes from a stall. White smoke billows up from her tiny stove.

The men burn their fingers peeling the potatoes, then devour them scorching hot. Pino wipes his fingers on the mop of hair beneath his soldier's cap and says, "We should go see Misangre."

"To get laid?" Aguado asks.

"No, to dig trenches!" Pino retorts. "Aguado, sometimes you're an idiot. Why else would we visit Misangre?"

Aguado shrugs.

"Okay."

Misangre's old brothel on Calle de Fielato, painted ocher yellow with blue trim, stands out from the chipped, peeling, abandoned homes around it. Outside waits a line

of soldiers of varying ranks—from sergeant on down—
and different forces: infantry, cavalry, artillery, even three
air-force mechanics. At the head of the line are a noisy
group of Italians from the Corpo Truppe Volontarie,
sporting their black braids, their black shirts and trousers,
daggers on their belts.

"Been waiting long?" Pino asks the last guy in line.

"Ten minutes, but this looks like it'll take a while."

"What's the holdup?"

"How should I know? Misangre probably lets the
Italians take their time, and then we're the ones who have
to go off like loaded pistols: Just aim and shoot."

Aguado looks at his watch.

"Know what I'm thinking? I don't want seconds."

"I might not mind seconds," Castro muses. "But who
knows how many times these dishes will have been passed
around before we get to the table?"

"Why don't we just go to the dance?" Pino asks. "Maybe
we'll get lucky."

"What dance?" Castro inquires.

"The second-company quartermaster told me there's a
baile de candil social dance on Calle de Enramadilla."

"Perfect," Aguado says. "We might meet some girls in
need of a little satisfaction."

"Castro and I would have to be the ones to give it to
them," Pino replies. " 'Cause you sure as hell can't—"

"Get your sister down here and you'll see," Aguado retorts, piqued.

"Enough," Castro intercedes. "Peace. Let's go to the dance."

Calle de Enramadilla is deserted: doors and windows shut, houses abandoned. One lone yellow rectangle of light shines from an open door at the end of the street.

"That must be it."

The building used to be a cabaret, back in the mine's heyday. They walk through the front door and cross a patio enclosed by a vine-covered arbor and stained-glass corridor. More light shines from the back: a large room decorated with beautiful, carved wooden caryatids, their breasts covered by a strip of wood that reads, *All praise and victory to our brothers from Germany, Italy, and Portugal, committed to our common goal of saving Christian Western Civilization from the clutches of atheist and dissolute Marxist Bolshevism. ¡Viva Franco! ¡Viva José Antonio! ¡Arriba España and her National-Syndicalist Revolution!* Despite the lengthy inscription, the last caryatid would have escaped censure and remained bare-chested had her breasts not later been concealed by a sloppy rendering of the Falange's yoke and arrows.

The soldiers enter the spacious room, vestiges of its luxurious past still evident, though the sheen on the banisters separating the raised area that was once reserved for elite clientele has faded. The ornate wrought-iron columns supporting the ceiling are hard to make out, too, in the dingy light of the weak bulbs covered with brass shades that have replaced the huge Murano crystal chandeliers. A cord, from which little red and yellow paper flags are suspended, runs the length of the room, from one column to the other.

The stage has remarkable baroque decor, most notably a profusion of mythological creatures that have all been covered up with long black strips of fabric stitched with the Spanish coat of arms and Saint John's eagle. On the back wall, a banner made of three sewn-together sheets proclaims, *El Caudillo, Generalísimo Franco, the invincible leader of the Heroic National Army, will defeat the Marxist–Leninist hydra and restore Imperial Spain to the glory and peace it once enjoyed.* Private areas are separated by a golden wood balustrade that runs the length of the room. Along with the enormous fresco on the ceiling depicting the rape of Europa—the old club was called Europa—these are the clearest signs of the place's former glory.

Back in the immoral days before the Crusade, miners used to throw back a few drinks while contemplating a naked woman with glimmering flesh riding a fighting bull at an improbable angle. The military *padre* who blessed the building ordered that the sinner be purified with a coat of whitewash, to cover her flesh from head to toe. While they were at it, they threw in a few extra brush-strokes to cover up the bull's big black testicles, which had been dangling provocatively like a couple of eggplants full of sperm.

"Who's that lady in the sack?" Castro inquires.

"A famous bullfighter who was born here." Aguado, as

usual, flaunts his expertise. "She'd dress up like the mata-
dor don Tancredo, and when the bull wasn't paying attention, she'd grab it by the horns and mount it."

"Now, that's one hell of a woman!"

The dance floor is big. Last winter its original planking
was pried up and burned for kindling, leaving a checkerboard of cheap terrazzo.

Things are starting to pick up. Husbands and wives as
well as groups of girls escorted by older women begin to arrive. Low-ranking soldiers saunter in by the dozen, merry
and jocular one minute, then momentarily solemn when
they pass a sergeant or second lieutenant. Respectable
older women—widows wearing scapulars and medallions
around their necks, each with her own cattail seat and a
sack of knitting and crocheting supplies—greet one another and take up position like sentries in the boxes from
which they keep watch over the dance floor and any potential hiding places. Before heading in, the young ladies listen attentively to their chaperones' orders.

"We're finished," Pino complains. "Here we are, selfless
military combatants, and those old bags are watching us
with eagle eyes."

"Well, what did you expect?" Aguado says.

"Me? I thought I might get laid."

"Real genius. Jack off before bed and you'll sleep like a
baby."

In a few minutes the orchestra arrives—four musicians
from the regimental band, plus a local with an accordion—

and takes its place onstage. They practice a few bars, then the leader stands and addresses the crowd. "Ladies and gentlemen, distinguished officers, with your permission, we are about to perform for you a *paso doble* called Sombrero, which my good friend Sergeant Martínez has requested."

He glances over at a short, dark, fat sergeant, who nods in recognition and raises a patrician hand to greet all present. The musician takes his seat, brings the clarinet to his lips, and nods at the others to strike up the music. Six or seven pairs of girls come out onto the floor, followed by a few married couples. Moments later other couples join them, under the close scrutiny of the chaperones, who've stopped sewing and chatting to concentrate on the dancers. Some of the girls feign resistance to please the gallery, then allow themselves to be dragged onto the floor. A row of girls sits before the band on folding chairs, giggling among themselves. Some impatiently keep time to the music with their feet.

After appraising the merchandise, young soldiers start asking girls to dance, the prettiest ones first. Some agree straightaway, persuaded by their friends; others play hard to get.

"So, Corporal, what do you think?" asks Pino, with a gleam of hope in his eyes.

"I've got my eye on that girl in the polka-dot dress with the square neck."

"I like the one next to her, the one with big tits."

Castro faces his friend. "What about you, Ramón?"

"I'm going to play it by ear; see how you make out first."

Pino shakes his head and sighs. "*Ay,* Aguado, you keep turning your nose up at women and you'll end up bending over for the soap!"

Castro and Pino straighten their army jackets, skirt the dance floor with their best military air, stiff and upright, stand at attention before a lieutenant in his forties—who looks resigned as he dances with a fat lady, possibly his wife—and reach the row of seated girls. Castro's mark, from up close, has pale skin and attractive features: Big honey-colored eyes gaze out from under carefully tweezed, arched brows; her nose is slightly snubbed; lipstick accentuates her fleshy, succulent lips.

He delivers the standard line.

"Would you be offended if I asked you to dance?"

Having studied him out of the corner of her eye since he first stood up, she responds, "No, I wouldn't be offended."

"Then may I have this dance, *señorita?*"

She glances at her friend, who's already accepted Pino's invitation and encourages her with a saucy wink.

"All right."

She stands, leaving her little raffia bag on the chair so no one will take her seat. Castro encircles her waist lightly, maintaining a safe distance. Her hand, soft and warm, is decidedly not the callused hand of a servant, sloughed with pumice stone.

Castro dances a decent *paso doble;* a couple of girlfriends in Lopera tried to teach him. He strives for an agility he doesn't possess. At first they dance in silence. She sees that the neck of his army jacket is caked in a thick layer of grime and black grease. The collar of his shirt, however, is noticeably cleaner, though faded after several attempts to boil the lice.

The corporal's face is coarse. His thick beard takes on a bluish tinge through his weather-beaten skin. He surreptitiously inhales her feminine scent. A clean woman, well scrubbed. He'd give anything to kiss those fleshy lips, that pearly-white neck. Suddenly he pictures casting a spell over the onlookers, putting them to sleep, even her. He'd throw her down on a table and really give it to her good. Shocked by his own morbid fantasy, he scolds himself. *Don't be a brute, Juan.*

"What's your name, *señorita?*"

"Concha. And you?"

"Juan Castro Pérez, at your service. You're a very good dancer."

"Where are you from?"

"La Quintería."

"Is that in the Canaries?"

"No, *señorita.* I'm serving with the Canaries Falange, but I'm from the mainland. La Quintería is a little farmstead near Andújar."

"But isn't that where the reds are?"

"It is, *señorita,*" replies Castro, careful to maintain his formal approach to the conversation.

"And your family? Are they safe?"

Castro lowers his head melodramatically. "I imagine they're out there. I haven't had news of them in two years." He's trying for compassion, attempting to gain her affections.

"Oh, I'm so sorry!"

"That's all right, *señorita*. What about you? Do you have family here?"

"You can call me Conchi," she responds, much to Castro's delight. "And yes. My parents run a hotel. Well, they did before the war. My father was manager of Hotel Paris, where the general staff headquarters is now. We've opened a *pensión* until things get back to normal. The Pensión Patria, in the plaza."

Castro feigns recognition. "Oh, yes! I passed by the sign earlier."

The *paso doble* has ended. The dancers let go of each other and head back to the row of seats. Some of the girls are now sitting in different places around the floor, chatting with boys under the vigilant eyes of their chaperones. Castro takes a seat beside Concha. Pino and the other young woman join them.

"This is my friend Pepi. Pepi, Juan," Concha introduces them.

"Pleasure."

"The pleasure's all mine."

The couples each take up their respective conversations

once more. Castro boasts to Concha that he's the son of a landowner, that his father has a medium-size farm engulfed in olive trees and a few wheat fields. Then as the conversation progresses, he even claims to own the horse he rides in the Virgin of Cabeza procession. Smart as a whip, his horse. He trained it to kneel before the Virgin. He enjoys hunting as well. He's won a few trapshooting championships with his Remington 29 shotgun.

Castro is not ashamed to pass himself off as *Señorito* Federico, the son of the Marquis of Pineda.

Concha remains thoughtfully silent after this revelation. Perhaps she's taking measure of him. Either way, she seems impressed.

"What do you hunt?" she asks, distracted.

"Oh, everything: deer, wild boar, hare, partridge..."

"You don't feel bad, killing all those beautiful animals?"

Castro wasn't expecting this, and he's thrown. He can't now confess that *Señorito* Federico actually does all the killing.

"Animals were created to be killed, right?"

Concha shrugs. "I'm not sure the animals feel that way."

Castro feels he's just lost all the points he'd stockpiled. He glances morosely at Pino, who seems to be doing just fine. Pepi's laughing with a brazenness that leaves no doubt she's caving. He's stroking her thigh discreetly. She pretends not to notice.

"Would you like to dance this one?"

Another *paso doble*. Concha thinks it over a moment before nodding with calculated indifference.

"All right."

They head back to the floor and dance in silence, their bodies a prudent distance apart.

Castro can't let it go. "I don't want you to think I really like hunting all that much. It's just that my father, my uncles…everyone hunts. Myself—I feel awful when a wounded deer gives you that desperate look."

Concha says nothing. She appears more interested in the music than in what he's saying.

Castro tries a new tack that has proved successful on other occasions. "I wish we could have met under other circumstances, not during the war."

"Why?"

"Oh, I don't know. It's like the war makes everybody go a little crazy." He looks into her eyes. "To tell the truth, I've never met anyone like you before."

She matches his gaze, stern. "Please! You don't even know me! You wouldn't recognize me if you passed me on the street tomorrow."

"Oh, I'd recognize you, all right."

She seems cross.

"Things are different for us," Castro reasons. "For soldiers, I mean. I'm here today, but tomorrow I'll be back in the trenches. Who knows if I'll make it out alive?"

Concha looks into his eyes again, alarmed this time.

"What makes you say that?"

"Oh, don't pay any attention to me. I had to have a couple of drinks just to get up the courage to ask you to dance. I'm very shy, you know."

"I'll bet you are!" She laughs, incredulous. "You, shy? I can see exactly what sort of cloth you and your friend are cut from."

"Him, maybe," Castro says defensively. "But I'm not like him."

"Well, I'm not like Pepi," Concha points out. "So don't get any ideas."

Castro and Concha look over at their friends, watch them stand, skirt the dance floor, and surreptitiously leave the room.

"Looks like they're getting on well," Castro says, not without envy.

"With Pepi, everything's easy," Concha observes, a certain edge to her voice. "Her boyfriend was killed last year, and she's still a little traumatized. But she's a good person," she rationalizes.

"What about you? Do you have a boyfriend?"

"If I did, I certainly wouldn't be here with you."

"I don't have a girlfriend either."

Concha smiles at that. "How do I know?"

"It's true!" Castro insists. "Why don't you trust me?" He smiles back.

"Because you're a soldier, and I know what soldiers are after. Particularly when they're on leave. You have one thing on your mind."

"Not me," Castro protests. "Or not with you, at least. You're different; you . . ." He searches for the word. "You impress me."

"I bet I'm not the first girl to hear that."

"Conchi, what do I have to do to make you believe me?"

She pauses to consider his request. "How long are you on leave?"

"I'm back in the trenches tomorrow," he replies dramatically.

"Will you write me?"

"I'm stationed in Cerro del Médico! It's right around the corner."

"It makes no difference where you are. I want you to write me a letter."

Castro quickly concedes. "Okay, then, I will. I'll write to you. But you have to give me your address."

"That's easy: Concha Rama Anula, Pensión Patria, Pueblonuevo."

"Then I'll write; I'll show you I'm serious."

They dance in silence until the song ends and people file back to their seats.

Concha looks at her wristwatch, bound by a little velvet strap.

"In seven minutes, it will be nine-thirty. I have to go home."

"Already?"

"Already."

"Can I walk you back?"

"What about your friend?"

Aguado, taking no interest in the dance, is chatting away in a box with two older women.

"He's a big boy," Castro says. "He'll make his way back to transit quarters when he sees I'm not here."

She thinks it over and then shrugs.

"Okay. If you want to."

It's chilly out. And dark. The stones glimmer in the faint glow of the lantern Castro carries. They walk in silence, a few feet apart, each lost in thought. He feels charged by the proximity of a female body, a woman who might hold the promise of intimacy if he handles the situation tactfully. He would have preferred a less conventional girl, one who'd have let him feel her breasts in some darkened alleyway, maybe go even further. A shiver runs down Castro's spine, and the stirring between his legs grows as he envisions caressing Concha's thighs, his fingers slipping between her legs to separate her lips, feeling her wetness. He cuts short the brazen fantasy. Concha's not like that, but he likes her anyway. He's going to write to her as soon as he gets back to Cerro del Médico.

When they reach the plaza, Concha moves even farther away, leaving a respectable distance between them. In front of the quartermaster's depot, Castro notices the sign for Pensión Patria for the first time. The door is closed.

Concha searches her bag for the key, slips it into the lock, turns, and says, "Thank you for walking me back, Juan."

"I'm going to write to you, you know," he reminds her. "And if I do, will you write back?"

"Why bother, if you're so close?" she jokes, whispering. "You write to me, and then we'll see."

Concha goes inside, but before closing the door she turns and says, "Good-bye, Juan."

"Good night, Concha." Castro holds out his hand, which she barely touches.

He stands at the closed door in a daze. Sniffing his hand, he takes in her light perfume and feels the shiver run down his back again, that familiar tightness brought on by contact with female skin.

"You're gorgeous, Concha," he whispers to himself, "and, God, do you make me hot."

Chapter 4

Castro heads to the transit quarters around the corner from the plaza, beside the town hall. He shows his leave papers to the guard on duty, a sleepy corporal who allows him through into a wide room with two rows of bunk beds occupied by soldiers, some snoring, others daydreaming.

He locates an empty bunk, a bottom one. Before getting in, he takes a few precautions: He rolls his infantry belt up and stuffs it into one of his boots, which he in turn stuffs between the mattress and frame, soles facing out, so he can rest his head on the legs. Then he climbs into bed fully dressed and pulls up a blanket. No one can rob him.

"We'll just have to deal with the bedbugs," he murmurs to himself.

"Shhh!" hisses the soldier in the next bunk.

"You there! Silence!" the reserve guard orders from over by the curtain.

"Guard!" a plaintive voice cries out from the darkness.

"What?"

"If you can guess what I have in my hand, I'll give you the leftovers."

"Would the comedians shut their traps?" another voice grumbles.

Corporal Castro unbuttons his fly to free his belly while he sleeps. Lying faceup, hands behind his head, he daydreams about the woman he just met. Concha Rama Anula. He thinks of Valentina.

"*Ay*, Valentina, I don't know who I love more, you or her. If I had my way, I'd take you both back to La Quintería."

He's drifting off when an unmistakable hoarse cough wakes him. Aguado is chatting in the doorway with the reserve guard on duty. Castro recognizes his boots beside the guard's rope-soled shoes in the square patch of light coming from under the curtain. Aguado steps into the dormitory, his flashlight aimed down at the floor.

"Pssst! Ramón! Over here!" Castro signals as quietly as he can.

Aguado takes his bearings.

"Where's Pino?" Castro whispers.

"Out somewhere with his hussy," Aguado responds.

Stripping off his uniform in two quick moves, he stands in his underpants and sniffs the sheets. He recons the bed with his flashlight, in search of bedbugs or the starchy remnants of ejaculate. Satisfied, he pulls them taut and spreads a couple of blankets out over the top.

"What about you? How'd it go?" Castro whispers. "Manage to shine your saber?"

"I ended up talking to a nurse at the field-dressing station, a real young one from Granada."

"And?"

The soldier who silenced him earlier is now alert, tuning in to the conversation.

"No shining," Aguado responds. "My dick was like a cannon ready to explode, but all she'd let me do was feel her tits." He tucks in the sheets and blankets. "She didn't trust me, and now I'll have to jack off. My balls are killing me."

"What did you say to her?"

"What do you think I said? Told her I'm rich. What the fuck else would I say?"

One of the lumps stirs in the corner of the room. "Shut up; we're trying to sleep!" he protests.

"Okay, let's go to sleep, man," Castro quips. "We're disturbing His Highness."

The next day, mid-morning, Castro and his muleteers return to the front.

Amor sees them jump off the truck and shouts, "Hey, look who it is! The studs are back, freshly fucked!"

"No, no," Pino jokes, "the whores were all in Belmez at a wedding, so we just had to jack off."

"Whose wedding?"

"Your sister's, you idiot," Aguado joins in. "You fall for it every time!"

Castro heads straight for the mules. Valentina is rooting through her trough. He strokes her hindquarters, her broad rib cage, her neck. She turns and recognizes him but pays no attention. Instead, she goes back to her fodder.

"Here we are again, Valentina! Did you miss me? Guess not, eh. Why would you—here at the trough, getting fat. You have no idea the lengths I go just to bring you half a peck of barley." He fingers the scab that's formed over the sore on her withers. "This is healing up real nice. Real quick. You can get back to work now, eh? Don't worry, though, I'll keep an eye out for you."

Heliodoro and Chato are smoking in the sun on the stone patio, sitting on a couple of packsaddles.

"Hey, get over here," Castro commands. "There's work to do! We got to water these animals."

They attach the animals' halters and form three trains. Castro follows last, staying back with Valentina.

"You and me are going to come out of the war just fine; they say it's almost over. We'll go back to La Quintería.

You'll love it, you'll see, it's nice out by the river, the grass so thick it's like walking on pillows. And I'll keep you happy until then; this barley's not so bad. You should have seen what it was like with the reds. We ate nothing but lentils. But here I eat meat stew, even though it's just mule—sorry. Don't worry: We only eat dead mules. We did earn ten *pesetas* with the reds, though; that much is true. But you tell me, what good is ten *pesetas* if there's nothing to spend it on?"

They reach the well, and Castro waits off to one side for the first trains to finish and move on.

"I hope you're going to fill up the trough for me," Castro warns his subordinates. "An old man can't go breaking his back, you know."

"What a *cabrón*!" Heliodoro replies. "Just because you're corporal, now you're an old man too? I cut my teeth in the army before you even got your uniform!"

"I'd already done my service; I started in '35."

Heliodoro and Chato finish watering their mules.

"Right; we're heading back to the *cortijo*."

"Go ahead, and when you get there tell the others to bring the rest of the mules. I'll stay here."

The muleteers head off. Castro frees his animals in the pasture by the trough. When he removes Valentina's head-stall, she gazes right at him with her big eyes and tosses her head, water dripping from the long hairs on her soft muzzle. Castro strokes it.

"This war hasn't been all bad, you know. Once I stuffed myself silly on ham—better than don Federico's ever eaten! It was last year, when I was on kitchen duty, in Utrera. Mmm, mmm! Got such a bellyache, I had diarrhea for three days."

Chapter 5

Years later, during Christmas vacations—when night fell slowly over La Quintería beneath a gentle rain—Castro would periodically recall the civil war. He'd relive his stories from this distant past, as if they'd taken place in another galaxy. He would remember Churri and the Peñarroya front, remember the adventures of his recruitment, time spent in boot camp, how he escaped to the nationalist side, and his exploits in Lopera, country towns, and Córdoba.

"A lot of things happened to me in the war. A lot of things happened to everybody. When the Falangist uprising first began, I'd already completed my military service as a *cuota* soldier in Granada, and I'd just been discharged when the war broke out. The *cuota* soldiers served less time, but we had to pay our own expenses and buy our uniforms. Don Federico, the marquis, paid my fees, for which my parents were grateful, though Churri came along later brandishing his Iberian Anarchist Federation armband, saying, 'You fool! Can't you see the marquis is only paying your fees because it's cheaper than paying a muleteer for the time you'd be off serving?' Maybe Churri was right, but don Federico had a good heart. Everybody was so poor back then, but we never wanted for anything in my house. My father—he was the groundskeeper and a sharecropper on the farm—pulled us through just fine, and we never went without a bottle of oil or a loaf of bread in the pantry. He worked hard, sure, but life is hard, right? And if you're born poor, you have to work, that's just the way it is. So I completed my service in Granada; sometimes while I was there I'd slip into civilian clothes and walk to the school by the Plaza del Triunfo to pick up girls, pretending to be a student.

"Once, when the churches were burned, they seconded us to a soldiers' platoon, gave us machine guns, and marched us up to the Sacromonte, in the hills above Granada, to protect the convent. Another time we were ordered to guard the Catholic Monarchs' theater, 'cause it seems they wanted to burn that too. But nothing terrible happened in Granada: The bad stuff came later.

"I was discharged on July first, 1936, and the war broke out just a few days after I got home. The night before

that, the sky itself was unbelievable. Shooting stars everywhere. Anyway, I was in La Quintería at the time, working
for the marquis, and they were calling up new columns
every few months. But I was at the bottom of the barrel;
even though I was a worker, they said I wasn't a leftist.
Then in March '37 they called *everybody* up, whether you
were on the right or the left. Didn't matter. They put us on
a train and took us to Albacete. You know why they called
us 'the sweet-tooth column'? 'Cause just about everybody
in the column was right-wing, so when we got to the front,
we were all thinking the same thing: desertion. And since
all we wanted to do was desert, they joked like it was
'dessert' and labeled us 'the sweet-tooth column' ever since.

"So there I was at the station with Chato, a shepherd
from El Lugar Nuevo. Poor guy, he was dumb as a stump.
And I said, 'Chato, what the hell are you doing here?'
'Well,' he said, 'the militiamen turned up the other day,
and what a mess it was. They took the goats, and they
took me too.' So we left together and he stuck by my side,
'cause that was the first time he'd ever been on a train, the
first time he'd been out of Andújar, and he was scared as a
rabbit in a wolf's mouth. So we both came over to the nationalists and stuck together during the whole war. Since
he never left my side, I used to call him my secretary, and
he'd laugh with that mess of yellow teeth of his. . . .

"We spent all night on the train in total darkness, unable to sleep through the recruits' singing. We only
stopped once after five hours—at some unmanned station

God knows where—to throw water on the engine. They let everybody off to piss and take a dump right by the on-coming tracks and gave us breakfast: half a crust of bread and a sardine each. Then it was back onto the train. That's how we spent the night. At dawn the next day we reached another station and they piled us into trucks headed for boot camp in Tobarra, a little town in Murcia, close to Jumilla. Wine country. And since we were in no rush to head out and be shot at, me and Chato deliberately failed training and spent three months in the idiots' company. But then they tested us at the firing range. The targets were one and two hundred meters away, but I was a pretty good shot 'cause I was used to assisting don Federico and the marquis when they went out hunting. And that was shooting left-handed, 'cause I've never seen too well out of my right eye. So they made me corporal machine gun-ner, gave me a gun, and taught me to use it. As a corporal, I got to hand-select a soldier to carry my weapon. Of course I picked Chato.

"After a month or so, they sent us to Jaén, to Andújar. You should have seen the whole family at the station, cry-ing! Everybody turned up. They all came out to see us in our uniforms—brand-new except for the boots. From Andújar we drove with the army to Arjonilla, where they took us to the Porcuna front, to a farmstead they call Torrealcázar—fortress tower—'cause there's an old Moors' tower there. We were the Hundred-sixth Mixed Brigade, five infantry companies. My mother visited me in Arjonilla to bring me a change of clothes, some chorizo, and other things my aunt Exupina had sent. She told me my father was being held prisoner by the nationalists in the Jaén cathedral. He wasn't hurt, just bored. The prisoners there passed the days playing cards they made out of parchment. 'Well,' I told my mother, when I knew no one could hear, 'I'm glad they haven't harmed him, but I'm crossing over to the nationalists as soon as I can.' My mother almost fainted. 'How could you?' she said. 'Don't you realize you could be shot for treason?' But she couldn't stop me. 'You think the reds won't kill me, too, once the first shots are fired? What makes you think any one of these men—and there are dozens from Andújar who know I'm right-wing—wouldn't shoot me in the back?' She seemed to see my point. 'Listen, Mother. When I send you a letter with a line through my signature, that means I'm about to go over. Don't answer that letter.'

"So my mother gave me a picture of the Virgin of Angustias, and that's how we left it. After a few days they sent me to the front, to the Torrealcázar trenches. As a precaution, the trucks painted their headlamps black, so the enemy couldn't see us, on the road or from the air."

Chapter 6

On September 12, 1938, Third Triumphal Year, His Excellency the Reverend Military Bishop of the Andalusian Army don Cosme Redondo Frajeiro is conducting a pastoral visit to the Peñarroya front, accompanied by a small entourage of servants, secretaries, photographers, and journalists. The objective of the prelate's trip is to hold an open-air Mass. The prelate is scared stiff by the war, which is why he's chosen a battlefield where a single shot hasn't been fired for weeks as his holy ground. (The action is all at the Battle of Ebro, more than five hundred miles from these trenches.)

In the Sierra Trapera, on the last stage of the journey, the mountains are steep, forcing the prelate to travel by mule. Commander Soler has named Juan Castro Pérez, corporal and master horseshoer, as the prelate's personal groom. For the occasion, the bishop will ride a mule known to be very docile, a mule Corporal Castro holds in very high esteem indeed: Valentina.

The episcopal delegation spends the night at a *cortijo* on the Duke of Siero's wild-game preserve, La Mariscala, currently uninhabited, as it is situated in the middle of the battlefield.

After foddering the mules, Castro breaks for a smoke in the farmyard, an abandoned garden now overgrown with thicket. In the center lies a circular stone slab upholding a dry fountain with the sculpture of a naked boy. Castro takes a seat on one of the tiled benches surrounding it and thinks of Concha, to whom he has written and will see again soon. He daydreams about going back to La Quintería after the war.

"You'll like it there, Valentina, going up to the shacks near the mine in Los Escoriales, chewing all that tasty grass.

"And you'll get to meet my cousin Oria." He smiles, thinking of her. "Her husband tended a herd of goats; good man . . . tiny little man, skinny guy, didn't talk much. One day he just hung himself, after milking the goats. Now Oria takes care of them, since she doesn't have any kids. When it rains, cousin Oria spends all day making cheese. I used to go watch her if I didn't have any chores, which wasn't very often. I'd help her add the rennet to the trough and she'd stir the milk with this giant spoon, just stir and stir until it hardened. Then she'd knead it in the big trough, and when the whey rose to the top and the curd stayed at the bottom, she'd make a ball and give me the leftover whey to drink in a tin jug. Then she'd cut it into pieces and press them into esparto molds, wrap straw around them, and put a plank on top, held in place by three or four stones that must've weighed—"

Castro starts, realizing he's not alone. A fat man in pajamas and a robe, whom he struggles to recognize as the army bishop himself, has appeared beside him.

"Your Reverence!" he exclaims, throwing down his cigarette and standing to attention as quickly as he can.

"Relax, son. Sit back down."

Castro tries to stamp out the butt.

"No need to stop smoking, son. Got one for me?"

"For Your Reverence?" Castro is shocked that a bishop might smoke, or perform any other mundane activity.

"Yes, son, for me."

Castro takes out his cigarette holder, mortified. "Your Lordship, all I have is loose black tobacco. Will that do?"

"Yes, it would. Go on and roll me a cigarette, son."

As the muleteer rolls the tobacco, squinting to make the most of the fading evening light, the bishop sits down on the opposite side of the bench, looking dejected.

"Here you are, Your Lordship."

The bishop lights the cigarette with the flint lighter the

muleteer holds out to him. Castro notes that the prelate's robe is closed: White chest hair peeks out over the top of it, and sweat glistens on his jowls. The bishop takes a deep drag, inhaling the smoke, and then exhales gently, blowing it up at the sky. He looks at the fountain's sculpture: a naked boy sitting on a rock, examining his foot.

"Fedelino," he murmurs.

"Pardon, Your Lordship?"

"That boy." The bishop points. "Fedelino. The boy with a thorn in his foot."

"Has Your Lordship been here before?"

The bishop laughs silently. "No, I've never been here," he declares, smiling sadly. "Fedelino is a famous sculpture. This is a copy."

Castro thinks about how many things a bishop must know that he does not.

The prelate takes a few more puffs, inhaling the smoke deep into his lungs.

"Black tobacco," the bishop says. "Poor quality, but there's something pure about it that I can't taste in the American cigarettes my nephew Pío sends. He's stationed at Red Cross headquarters in Burgos." He pauses. "Where are you from, son?"

"Jaén."

"And how's the war going?"

"Can't complain as of yet, Your Lordship. We're doing all right."

The prelate takes another deep drag and, his voice hoarse, as if he were talking to himself, asks, "What do you know about God?"

Castro turns to him, befuddled. "The Lord?"

"Yes, God."

"I . . . I'm sorry," Castro begins. "Not much, Bishop. I know He died on the cross for our sins and that He's helping us win the war from up in heaven. Right?"

The bishop nods. "Yes, from up in heaven He's helping us win this Crusade, this Holy War. And tell me, when I raise my hands during the holy sacrifice at Mass, do you believe the wine turns to blood, the blood of our Redeemer, and the bread becomes His flesh? Do you truly *believe* it?"

"Sir," Castro responds, confused, "I'm an ignorant soul. I took my first Communion at fourteen when I went to town to buy bread. We lived on the farm, and my uncle's wife—Benita was her name, a devout woman, very pious—saw me with a little donkey and told me, 'Come here, nephew, you're going to take your first Communion.' She gave me an armband and lent me one of my cousin's clean shirts and walked me to church immediately. The priest came in and gave me Holy Communion. But I don't know much about doctrine, Your Lordship."

The bishop listens in silence.

"And what are you doing here with the nationalists, if you're from the red zone?"

"I switched sides, Your Lordship," Castro replies, pride welling up.

"You switched sides? But you're poor."

"Yes, Your Lordship, poor but right-wing."

"A poor right-winger!" the bishop reflects. "That's good. So you don't believe in the socialist revolution."

"No, Your Lordship. Yours truly is a man of order. My family is very happy serving the Marquis of Pineda. The reds jailed my father for it. Before the war, I had a friend who used to talk total equality, how nobody has a right to exploit anybody else, but he never convinced me. Maybe they went hungry at his house, but under the marquis's protection, we always had food on the table."

The prelate observes the soldier, intrigued.

"I'm from a poor family too," he says, almost to himself.

"Your Lordship is?"

"Yes. And I, too, had a marquis who paid my fees at the seminary. I was saved from a life of callused hands," he says, pointing to Castro's rough hands, "and from going hungry like your friend."

"My friend used to say that priests are all smoke and mirrors. They convince the poor that they'll be better off when they die, so they won't rebel against the men who exploit them here on earth. They wash their hands of sorrow and poverty, that's what he used to say."

"And what do you think?"

"I don't think anything, Your Lordship. There's always been rich and poor."

"Smoke and mirrors..." the bishop murmurs, contemplating the white trail rising from the cigarette in his hand.

Castro feels uncomfortable. He wants to retreat to the barn with the other soldiers guarding the episcopal entourage, but he thinks it disrespectful to leave before the bishop. So he continues to sit, knees together, hands on his thighs, not daring to glance over at the prelate in his pajamas and robe.

"And when you're in danger, when bullets are whizzing past you—do you feel scared? What do you think about?" the bishop inquires.

"Your Holiness, when you hear bullets whiz past, it's because they've passed; the ones that kill you, you never hear. When it's heavy artillery and you see the cannon blasts approaching, all you can do is hide your head in a hole. That's scary."

"And what do you do? Do you find strength in God?"

Castro hesitates before answering. "No, Your Holiness, I think of my mother and how mad she'd be if I got killed."

The prelate nods.

"Go on now, son. Go with God."

Castro gets up quickly and stands at attention.

The bishop blesses him and holds out his ring, which Castro kisses.

"Good night, son. See you tomorrow."

Chapter 7

Pueblonuevo, September 17, 1938
Third Triumphal Year

Dear Juanito,

I'm writing to you after our walk together this afternoon, the memory of every thing you said fresh in my
mind, and I feel flattered and worried at the same time.
If your sentaments are all true, then I'm very exited, because just like any women, what I want is to find a
man who loves me.

But you're sincerity fritens me, since we barely even
know each other yet and haven't spent much time

together. I don't hardly know anything about you, or you about me. My heart tells me that your a good man but that's all I can say for now since affection and happiness come with more time.

Does that make sense to you?

Days ago, when you plucked that leaf off a tree and told me you were going to save it for the rest of your life as a momento, I have to say I was moved. My heart told me to speak clearly to you, to open up and be sincerely, but I just couldn't do it. My sentaments are so mixed up that I don't know how to explain them—I don't even know what's happening or what I feel my self, all I know is that when I tried to be honest and open up I couldn't because its like I cant catch my breath.

This is all so strange! That I can't explain it!

Over the years, since I became a young lady, I have had several sutors and it was always very easy for me to turn them away, but with you I cant because I don't know what to make of all your attentions.

As far as you're character is concerned, I have discovered that in the time you've been here you went out with another girl who I don't know but I've heard about her and that's what really scares me—that you've only just gotten to know me and yet already you said all those things. Anyway, I want to believe that your not one of those boys who just wants to go out with a girl to have a good time because if that was true you should know that I am definately not one of those girls whose there for a good time. What I'm looking for is something serious and committed. So if that's the case than I can tell you right now don't come see me any more don't come to meet me and we can just be friend's. I'm sorry I have to say these things but you know what its like right now, and because of the war people act different and things happen and I just don't want to be decieved. You know that with so many boys on the lose in a town with so few girls that there's forty who are just looking for a good time for every one whose serious about things and they'll lie and then after a few days act like they never saw you in their life. Its never happened to me of course but you hear a lot of things at the pensión and you learn a lot from those stories.

If I really mean something to you, please don't rush me besides when a man really loves a woman he will wait for her as long as it takes.

That thing Pepi said about you not being my type was just nonsense so don't listen to her because I can tell you that I think your fine, I'm not a verse to you and anyway I'm not hoping to marry some Rudolph Valentino and I'm not a silly girl who's got her head-filled with stories so if I am going to love you one day then I'll love you like you were the only man on earth, which is how I was taught a women should love.

From what you've told me about your family I

would not be out of place because in my family even though we're a modest middle class family I have an education and know how to cook and sew and keep house and no one would have to teach me anything and all though I might not be as cultured as your family I wouldn't be out of place because as you can see by this letter I'm modest and my conduct is always proper. I don't aspire to marry a wealthy man but a man who will love me and allow me to make him happy to. I know that men consider me beautiful and that's why more than one has paid me complaments but I hope your not one of those and that your more sincere than them. I'm only saying that because this afternoon you paid me so many complaments its not that I don't like flattery but sometimes I think you might just be a talker and I wonder how many girls you've said that to.

Please don't show this letter to anybody, even your very best friend in the world because you know how everybody talks and then things get out of hand and I don't want anybody talking about me.

Conchi

I salute Franco!
¡Viva José Antonio Primo de Rivera!
¡Arriba España!

Chapter 8

Castro's getting sacks of barley from the battalion storehouse. For some time now, he's been using any excuse to go to Peñarroya, so he can see Concha. Like a child alternating between parents, Castro seeks permission at times from Lieutenant Rufo and other times from Lieutenant Vico, so they won't notice how often he's away from the front. But this time he's been found out.

"You think you're on fucking vacation?" Lieutenant Vico yells. "If you can't get by without getting laid, then you can jack off like every other poor fuck around here. Next time you turn up missing, you're going to be in such deep shit that not even the Virgin of Pompillo will be able to dig you out. Is that clear?"

"Yes, sir."

This has not been Castro's day. Luisa, the maid, just told him that Concha went to Córdoba with her mother to buy sheets for the hostel. Annoyed, Castro lands himself in the cantina. He's just been served a glass of wine when the gunsmith's assistant comes to inform him they've repaired a machine gun that he is to take back to Commander Bozal of the first company.

"Sure, man, makes no difference to me. What's one more thing to deliver? Andalusian messenger, that's me."

When he goes to pick it up, leading Valentina by the halter, he bumps into Commander Arenas's liaison.

"Castro, you have a passenger. Commander's orders."

"What passenger?"

"A new second lieutenant being posted to your company."

Castro shrugs. "Well, at least we'll have company for the trip."

"Who's 'we'? Aren't you alone?"

"No, I've got animals here, plus Valentina."

"*What?* There's a *woman* in the trenches?"

"No, Valentina's a mule, *cabrón*. But she's got more sense than you."

"Good God, the things you hear," the liaison murmurs as he ambles off. "Half of them have lost their minds, with all this shelling."

———

The second lieutenant is twenty-one years old. His name is José Estrella Alpuente. He's from Madrid but was on vacation at his uncle's in Málaga when the war broke out. When the city was freed, he was drafted and sent to the academy. He tells Castro his story as they're making their way up the Aljibejo trail on Pajares Hill. Castro wonders if the academy didn't also teach him to keep his distance with the troops. But Estrella seems like a nice kid. Probably just needs to get it out of his system; it happens to everyone when they're first sent to the front. Once they reach Cerro del Médico, Estrella will find company with Second Lieutenant Moncada and Lieutenant Vico; soon he'll be pretending not to recognize Castro, looking the other way when they bump into each other, regretting he ever told him anything about his life.

"How about you? Where're you from?"

"La Quintería, sir. From a farmstead near Andújar, though I've lived most of my life on my master's farm in the Sierra Morena."

"Your *master*?"

"The Marquis of Pineda, don Federico Cañabate Díaz de Quesada, sir. You've never heard of him?"

"Why would I have?"

"He's only one of the richest men in Spain! He had three cars and twenty mule teams."

"What happened to him?"

"He escaped, thank God, just when the reds started

shooting people. He was able to get his family out to their house in Bia ... Bia ..."

"Biarritz?"

"That's it! In France. I can never get the name right. Anyway, they got out just in time. The next day the militias got to Los Escoriales and made off with everything: animals, wheat, oil, tools, the whole lot. They even took the furniture. They left a guard at the house and jailed my father—he's the marquis's groundskeeper—for being a fascist."

"And how did you manage to escape?"

"I just kept working at the people's cooperative they had set up at Los Escoriales. But after they drafted me into the 'sweet-tooth column,' I crossed over to the nationalists and never looked back."

When Second Lieutenant Estrella was a student in Madrid, he used to attend leftist political meetings and even considered joining the Socialist Youth. In his last year of college, his father gave him the Royal Academy of the Language dictionary, and the first thing he did was cross out the word *Royal* on the cover and sketch the republican crown over the royal one on the coat of arms, to the great distress of his right-wing Christian family. He liked Castro, identified with him. A declassed worker so used to his indentured state that he goes over to the other side to join his exploiters and is happy in his ignorance.

They carry on in silence until suddenly the distant droning of a plane echoes through the sky. Castro stops and holds an arm out before the second lieutenant's chest, barring his way.

"Sir, we don't know whether that bird is one of ours or one of theirs. We better take cover in the brush."

He disperses the mules behind the trees, personally escorting Valentina and the second lieutenant under the thick foliage. He strokes Valentina's neck.

"You just take it easy, baby." He turns to the second lieutenant and explains, "It'll fly over any minute. If the pilot sees us, he might spray us just for the hell of it. Real bastards; they have it out for the mule trains."

The aircraft—a reconnaissance biplane—comes into view. They can make out black circles beneath the wings; the tail sports the nationalist air force's black cross on white background.

"Don't the mules get spooked?"

"These mules? No way! They've seen more action than 'Cascorro' González in the Cuban war! And Valentina here's got more sense than most people. Mules are the most reliable animals in the world, in case you didn't know. They have a higher tolerance for fatigue than horses. See those hooves? They're small, and their gait is low to the ground, so they're sure-footed on rocky trails; you wouldn't believe the uneven trails we suffer to transport the *nicanoras*—those are Schneider mountain cannons, sir—and munitions to the trenches. Plus, mules don't eat much and can survive a hard day's work with no water. Besides, look here: Their backs and loins are straighter than horses', and when they're tethered together they're strong as hell. Perfect beasts of burden."

The second lieutenant seems more concerned with the plane.

"Don't worry, sir, he's on our side," Castro says to calm him, "but we'll wait 'til he flies off, 'cause from that high up, he can't tell whether we're nationalists or reds." The second lieutenant remains silent. "You know anything about planes, sir?"

"Not much."

Castro remains pensive.

"Once, when I was a kid, I was out with the pigs in a place called Las Viñas, and a zeppelin flew over. You know what a zeppelin is, sir?"

"Of course."

"Huge thing, sir. Unbelievable. So majestic. That motor humming, slowly pushing it along . . . It must've taken half an hour to disappear over toward Córdoba. Later I found out it was carrying passengers, luggage and all, to Sevilla. I just don't understand how anything that big could *float*."

Second Lieutenant Estrella laughs heartily. "That's easy, man! The top, the cylinder, is full of a gas lighter than air. You ever seen those balloons they sell at fairs, the ones that if you let go of the string, they float off?"

"Yes, sir."

"Well, that's because anything lighter than air floats."

He eyes Estrella suspiciously. "You pulling my leg?"

"Not at all. In a zeppelin, they put that gas in an aluminum and oilskin frame, and it floats up. Underneath it there's a basket; that's where the people go, with their luggage."

Castro stares solemnly at the second lieutenant. "Knowledge is an amazing thing, sir. The information you must have in your head ..."

"You can learn just about anything in books, Corporal. Nothing mysterious about it."

The plane disappears into the horizon. Castro looks up at the clear sky.

"We can go now, sir. The Mosca's gone."

They complete the rest of their journey in silence. Castro laments the fact that he's never read any books, particularly because don Federico had a whole roomful of them, floor to ceiling, at Los Escoriales. He thinks of his friend Churri, to whom he used to sneak the marquis's books, on secret loan. He wonders if Churri managed to escape the war, if he's still alive.

They reach the Valsequillo road.

"That first hill there is Cerro del Médico, sir, where the company has dug our trenches. The command post is behind those holm oaks. If you have no objection, sir, I'm going to get this gun over to the first company."

"Fine, Castro. I hope to see you around. We'll share a glass of wine."

As Castro salutes, Estrella holds out his hand. After

hesitating for a moment, Castro takes it. These academy greenhorns don't know you're not supposed to get friendly with the troops. He'll learn soon enough.

"Good luck, Lieutenant, sir."

Castro heads off, Valentina and the other mules ambling behind single file, and the second lieutenant watches fondly after him and says to himself, "If anyone were ever to enlighten him as to how society really works, the way I'd just explained the zeppelin, he'd join the side of justice." Estrella pauses to reject the notion. "Don't play savior; now's not the time for indoctrination. The minute that bumpkin sees your true colors, he'll report you. He'd deliver your head on a platter in exchange for a leave."

Chapter 9

Castro has been seeing Concha for a month and a half. He's resolved to purchase a pair of earrings to give her, proving his commitment to their relationship. He seeks his friend Sergeant Major Gil at the company office to request leave.

"He's been relieved of duty," the clerk informs him.

"Did he take a hit in yesterday's bombardment?"

"No, no. He went to get his picture taken for a girl and he pulled his belt so tight over his belly that he ended up with a hernia."

"Jesus! That's a shame."

"Yeah, but you should've seen the photo: He looks forty pounds lighter, his stomach's sucked in, and he touched up his hairline with burnt cork so you can't even tell he's balding."

"What about his nose?"

"Still looks like a squashed tomato. The photographer couldn't do anything about that."

Castro leaves the hut deflated. His company has been reinforcing their positions along the Sierra Patuda recently, and there's a lot of work for the muleteers. If Sergeant Major Gil can't pull strings for him, there's no point tempting fate with Lieutenants Vico and Rufo; they've already got their backs up over his trips to Peñarroya.

Suddenly, he gets an idea.

"Second Lieutenant Estrella! Of course!"

He asks Estrella for permission to visit the souk.

"To buy some earrings?"

"Lieutenant, sir, I'm not going to lie to you. They're for Concha. I'm trying to soften her up."

The second lieutenant ponders for a moment.

"Well, we could say you're buying ointment for the animals."

The souk is in Tres Mojones. Fifteen or twenty Moors from the Moroccan platoon defending Nava Redonda, near Villanueva, set up miserable little stands there every Thursday morning to sell provisions and secondhand goods. War booty.

Castro knows one of the merchants, a young Moor named Mohammed. He's wearing a jacket and baggy trousers, exposing an almond-colored complexion, shaved head, bony face, and big teeth. His left foot is missing; shrapnel blew it off a year ago during the taking of Obejo.

"Hey, Mohammed, business hopping?" Castro asks wryly, by way of greeting.

"Mohammed hopping, *cabrón!*" the Moor replies, donning his best obsequious smile, flashing a mouthful of wolfish yellow teeth, a chip on his first molar. "Happy to see you, my friend. You buying? I have everything, Corporal. You want good chicken?"

"No, I don't want a chicken."

"No chicken! Never mind. I have everything, my friend: good eggs, baby lotion, tobacco for smoking, chocolate for eating, rubbers for fucking, papers for smoking, papers for writing, flint for lighters..." The Moor reels off the products lined up on his blanket one by one.

Castro looks at the unrolled condoms, scraps of newspaper stuffed inside to keep them from sticking together.

"Those rubbers reliable?" he asks, pointing to them.

Castro has learned that, in order to barter with Mohammed, he first has to show an interest in something he doesn't intend to buy.

"Rubbers?" Mohammed dons a naughty smile and wags a finger, as if to scold Castro. "Ah, ah, my friend! I like you. You know what I'll do? For you, I've got very reliable rubbers. Italian, thoroughly washed with good vinegar. Very reliable. One *peseta,* one rubber. Good, cheap, and the best."

"One *peseta*?" Castro feigns indignation. "I'll give you five *céntimos,* and you can count yourself lucky!"

"You're crazy, man. For five *céntimos* you'll fuck with nothing and get the clap. Go to the hospital, make a doctor put a needle in your dick. Hurts! You're cocky now, but when you're in the hospital, you'll think of your friend Mohammed. . . ."

"No way, man. For that price I'll beat off, thanks! What about earrings? You got any earrings?"

Mohammed crouches down, exposing filthy, bony knees, and smooths out the rubbers, mulling over the question.

"Castro, I have everything you need, good and cheap. What's earrings?"

Castro pinches his earlobes. "What women hang here."

"Ah!" Mohammed exclaims. "Okay! You want earrings? Pretty earrings?"

"Yes."

"Well. Jewelry. That's serious. You got *pirra*?" he asks.

"What's *pirra*? Speak plain Spanish, man."

"Pirra, pesetas, reales . . ."

"Money? Yeah, I got money."

"Wait one moment."

Mohammed hobbles off to another stall a little farther down, by the riverbed. He throws his arm around a fat Moor, who turns to look at Castro and nods at Mohammed's Arabic, dips a hand into the depths of his baggy trousers, and extracts a bundle tied loosely in a dirty handkerchief.

He unties four knots and spreads it open, the contents in his cupped hand. It contains, among other things, a few jewels and a handful of gold teeth that have been yanked from dead soldiers' mouths. He hands Mohammed two earrings. The crippled Moor returns to Castro.

"My cousin has beautiful earrings. You're lucky: I've told him you're a good friend, a good customer. We'll sell them to you cheap: one hundred *pesetas*."

"You want twenty *duros:* a hundred *pesetas*? You're crazy, Mohammed! I'll give you twenty-five *pesetas* and we'll have a deal."

"You're robbing me, Corporal! You have no heart! I have five babies in Morocco; we're a poor family! Eighty *pesetas!*"

"No, siree, Mohammed, no way. Thirty *pesetas,* tops."

"Thirty *pesetas*? Two earrings, good gold, good stones? You're killing me, Corporal. I'm genuinely offended. Seventy-five *pesetas,* cheapest price!"

"Thirty-five, that's my highest offer."

"Sixty!"

"Forty!"

"Fifty!"

Castro grunts. "Fifty."

He takes out his wallet and gives Mohammed the money, two twenty-five-*peseta* bills. Mohammed examines them, checks the watermarks, ensures they're not counterfeit, then crumples them up into a tight wad that he slips into the folds of his baggy trousers.

"You're robbing me, Corporal! You got no pity for my children," he protests, wrapping the earrings in newspaper that Castro immediately reopens. He pockets the earrings in his army jacket.

"See you around, Mohammed."

"How about a sewing machine? Cheap?"

"No thanks."

Castro is happy with his purchase. He ambles off, Mohammed's voice trailing after him.

Chapter 10

The muleteers are happy. Having delivered the last load of *nicanoras* and boxes of ammo to their positions on the Cruz mountain pass, they've been granted a day's leave. After a lunch of rice and salt cod, they're passing around the wineskin. Heliodoro and Amor break into a soldier's song, the *"Carrasclás,"* which the others echo.

> On the road to Valsequillo
> You can see the streetlamp glow
> And there's a sign that tells you
> Fuck yourself and then go home!
> *Carrasclás, Carrasclás...*
> What a lovely serenade!

Carrasclás, Carrasclás
How I wish I'd never stayed

Castro pisses in the platoon latrine out in the holm oaks. Instead of returning to the scrub fire, he walks off behind some crags to protect himself from the north winds, sits on the ground with his back against a kermes oak, pulls Concha's last letter from the upper pocket of his army jacket, and reads, for the fifth time:

Pueblonuevo, November 30, 1938
Third Triumphal Year

Dear Juanito:

I have to beg your pardon for not responding since your last letter. It is nothing more then a flaw of my character. Since you said you had a sort of girlfriend back in Andújar it ocurrs to me that maybe your even married and just hiding it from me. I feel your such a good friend that this could become something deeper if I can believe what you tell me. I don't know why I keep thinking like this but I do, what can I say. Women can just tell with things like that sometimes. Its part of our intuition. I don't want to make you sad by telling you this because if I didn't want to trust you and wasn't interested in you I wouldn't even write. But if you love me then you'll be patient, because that's how you show true love, and I'm not interested in one of those war time affairs. You know what I mean. I don't want anybody to play with my feelings. Do you really love me? Your not lying?

I can tell you, in all honesty, that I am not a verse to you and whats more, I am in a fight with Pepi because the other day she said to me I don't know what you see in him, you always like tall blonds and he's neither one nor the other.

Do you think if I didn't like you I'd let you come see me and take me for walks? That makes sense to you doesn't it?

And now I have to ask you a question. If I one day love you and my parents object will you fight for me? I think when my parents find out that your serious they won't object but I have to know.

Anyway I'm not going to write anymore right now because I imagine you don't have time to waste. I hope you can write to me tonight so you can give me your letter next time I see you.

With sincere affection,
Conchi

I salute Franco!
¡Viva José Antonio Primo de Rivera!
¡Arriba España!

Chapter 11

December 2, 1938. It rained all night. A faint light on the horizon heralds a murky dawn. Castro sits up on his straw mattress, sticks his head through a hole in the middle of his blanket cape, and ties it to his waist with a cord. He rouses the other muleteers with his foot, kicking those who are sound asleep.

"Rise and shine, babies, the sun's up and there's work to do; time to earn your daily bread for Spain!"

They grumble as they rise slowly, sleepily, their limbs numb from the cold, aching from the lumpy beds.

The fire they burned all night in the middle of the shed has been reduced to a pile of smoldering ash. Cárdenas and Petardo go out to look for firewood in the damp gray mountain mist.

It's raining again. Aguado returns from the kitchen with their breakfast: one crust of bread and an old strip of bacon each, plus two cups of chicory per head. It's a long walk back, and the chicory has gone cold already. Before serving, Pino puts the milk churn on the fire he's just lit.

"What a shitty day! I wish those fuckers would just leave and the damn war would end already...."

Petardo, tall and skinny, digs around in his armpit, examines his fingernail, and discovers a louse. He traps it carefully and flings it into the fire.

"This is heaven, Pino. They're a lot worse off up there than we are down here," he says, pointing toward the Mano de Hierro positions. "Yesterday, when I took their mail up, I found Commander Camuñas shivering in his blanket and half a dozen recruits bailing water out of their hut with tin cans. Half the roof had collapsed and the whole place was flooded. They were up to their ankles in shit."

"In Obejo, man, that's where it really rained on us," Cárdenas recalls. "There was nowhere to hide back there. The water just streamed down your face to your shirt, down your chest and back; you had to undress so it wouldn't go down your pants, 'cause if you get a chill in your kidneys, you've had it."

"Well, if you think with the life we're leading here we're

not going to be full of aches and pains, you've got another think coming," Heliodoro says. "Wait and see what old age has in store for us."

No one speaks. Castro thinks, *For those of us who reach old age, that is.* He keeps his mouth shut, though. Now that he's corporal, he's taken on the commanders' habit of silencing any thoughts that might demoralize the troops.

Aguado takes the top off the churn and sticks his finger into the liquid. It's hot. He pulls it off the fire.

"Quick, before it gets cold."

They hold out their cups, which are tins of condensed milk with the lids bent back into improvised handles, and Aguado ladles out the steaming-hot murky liquid. Some of the men crumble their bread into their cups and eat the mush with spoons.

"It's better with milk," Pino says. "Next week we got to ration it better, 'cause the new quartermaster's a tight-wad who won't give out anything the sergeant doesn't tell him to."

"Oh, he'll soften up as soon as he needs the mules for something."

"In Obejo," Cárdenas remembers, "we killed one of those militiawomen who throw dynamite. You know, the ones who make bombs out of old tins full of wire and nails and shrapnel they find by the trenches." Cárdenas imitates her movements. "That little commie raised her arm but was shot before she could throw one at us. She dropped the bomb. The fuse was too short and it blew her up on the spot. By the time we got to her, she was already dead, a total mess. You could see her whole rib cage; half her head was gone, but her face was all there. I tell you, she was gorgeous. What I wouldn't have given to find her alive!"

Castro, Pino, and Aguado go out to the stables.

"So what's this I hear about you having a girlfriend?" Aguado asks.

"Something like that."

"They're all snakes, you know. I just hope this one isn't poisonous."

"You're not in love with me, are you, Aguado?" Pino says. " 'Cause it sure seems that you don't like women."

Aguado shrugs but makes no reply. His eyes glaze over. "I think about my life before I became a soldier; it's something I keep to myself. Whatever I think about women is none of your business. Fool."

Although the rain's coming down in buckets, they receive an order to transport supplies to the company. Trucks have dropped off impedimenta in the orchard in Rincón: tiles, asbestos sheeting, and boxes of little Italian Breda grenades, which the soldiers refer to as "oranges." The drivers load up their mules and start their long, arduous journey to their positions. Castro supervises the delivery and requests the signatures of those in charge—Captain Cobo in Gamonal and Lieutenant Ramírez in Cansino— when he runs into Second Lieutenant Estrella.

"How's it going, Castro?"

"Fine, Lieutenant. I'm the courier of the czar! Can't have enough *nicanoras* and hand grenades."

"You picked quite a day to deliver, in this rain."

"That's up to the commander. Perhaps so the planes can't see us. . . . It really is something, eh? I hope summer hurries up; I'm ready to bake in the sun."

"And how are things with your girlfriend?"

"Fine, sir. I gave her those earrings and she loved them, just like you said. But then she sent the maid to tell me she wouldn't come to the dance with me that night."

"How come?"

"Seems the earrings had some blood on them. She thought the Moor who sold them to me had snatched them off some red."

"Castro! Christ, man, how could you not have washed them before you gave them to her?"

"Lieutenant, sir, I thought they were okay. You know women, they look at every little detail—they notice those things."

Lieutenant Estrella shakes his head. "Did she give them back to you?"

"No. She didn't go that far."

"Good, then you're fine. Just write her a letter—tell her that it's not your fault, that you weren't about to ask the Moor where he'd gotten them. And, Castro, if you clean them with alcohol, the stains will wash right off."

"Do you think you could write the letter for me, sir?

You have a way with words, a remarkable skill. If you'd do that for me, I'd be in the clear."

"All right, Castro, but I'm not guaranteeing any results."

"Can't be worse than if I did it, sir, that's for sure."

Chapter 12

December 3, 1938. Third Triumphal Year. Second Lieutenant Estrella finds Corporal Castro at the Peñarroya barracks.

"What are you doing here, Castro? Still ducking out of work?" the officer jokes.

"I'm here for horseshoes and medication for the animals, Lieutenant, sir."

"And I'm here to collect my company wages," Estrella says. "But they're not available until tomorrow. Did you already visit your girlfriend?"

Castro blushes faintly. "No, sir. Mondays she goes to Córdoba with her father, to buy food for the *pensión*."

"Free as a bird, then," Estrella observes. "Let me buy you a glass of wine at Terrible's Club."

"Okay."

After sharing half a liter of red at a table near a heater, the soldiers begin their walk back to their respective lodgings at Plaza Peñarroya: the second lieutenant in the officers' residence, Castro in the transit quarters. The weather clears and the cold lets up.

"Castro, how was it that you came over from the reds?"

"It's a long story, sir."

"What's the rush?"

"No rush, sir. If you want to hear it, I'll tell you." Castro pauses to jog his memory. "Last year they took me to the Porcuna front, on July fifth, to a place called Torrealcázar, between Porcuna and Pilar de Moya. Our first night they sent us to the side of a hill to sleep in huts covered with camouflage canvas, and when day broke, we had breakfast, then headed off to the trenches. When I reached my company, I asked an old man where the nationalists were positioned. 'Right over there, to the right of Porcuna.' He pointed. 'See that little hill?' They were probably five kilometers away. 'They can't shoot this far, but I'll be damned if the cannonfire don't make it!' he said.

"I'd already talked to six others about going over to the nationalists—we were all right-wing—so I found them and proposed, 'The minute anybody goes over to the enemy, they're going to start watching us like hawks, so we have to be the first to do it, tomorrow, as soon as it gets dark.' Since I was corporal, I put three of my own men on sentry duty that night. So when night fell and it was all quiet on the front, the three sentinels and me crawled through a hole in the fence. Chato fell into a ditch full of empty cans and dry sticks—made more racket than a donkey on a roof." Castro smiles. "With so many new recruits on the front—guys who get spooked at anything—they thought it was a nationalist attack and started shooting like crazy. One of our men got lost and was caught, and eventually it was just me and Chato left running.

"I don't remember if I told you this before, Lieutenant, but Chato's from Andújar like me, a poor kid from the sierra. I put him to work as a mule driver in the third company; he follows me around like a puppy. He'd jump into a well if I asked. That's how loyal he is; really looks up to me. His real name's Manuel Gutiérrez Cano. The son of coal sellers. Whenever he was out hunting in the mountains, he used to come by Los Escoriales, to the Marquis of Pineda's game reserve, where my family works, and my mother would give him a few slices of meat in a tin can. You could say she just about raised him; he'd have been a skinny little runt if it wasn't for her. Those coal sellers, they lived like animals, entire families in the same shack, parents and children sleeping in the same bed. What little they made from selling charcoal at the market, they'd spend on cognac; they'd about forsaken their kids.

Anyway, so that day all the shooting broke out. Chato and me took off like colts, scared to death, bullets flying every which way. Luckily, it was a dark night and the recruits couldn't shoot for shit. By the time they lit up the whole camp with a flare, me and Chato had already sprinted five hundred meters and were hiding in a ditch. You wouldn't believe how fast we ran!"

The second lieutenant takes out his silver cigarette case and offers Castro a Bisonte cigarette. Castro feels for his lighter, gives the second lieutenant a light, and then lights his own cigarette. After taking a drag, he continues with his story.

"When things calmed down and they stopped firing, I knew we had to get out of there. Chato agreed. So we headed off into the olive trees, Chato scared witless, scared that every tree was a red soldier. And after walking for ages, when I thought we'd almost reached the nationalist trenches, I said, 'Chato, we gotta wait 'til first light so they can see us and don't shoot.' So we went into a hollow, too nervous to sleep, and when day broke I saw the Torrealcázar tower right there in front of me. I looked back and saw Porcuna off in the distance. I couldn't fucking believe it! We got turned around in the dark and we were back where we started!" Estrella laughs heartily. "And Chato suggested that we claim we got lost hunting asparagus. 'Shit, Chato,' I said, 'don't be an idiot. How can we be out hunting asparagus when it's not even in season? Snails, maybe.'

"So we snuck out of the olive trees and headed off to find a ravine with a few good trees for cover. I said, 'What we gotta do is wait here all day, and when it gets dark, we'll go over to the nationalists.' And after a while, some muleteers came by to fetter their animals in the pasture; we just sat tight so they couldn't see us. And we waited all day, dying of thirst, not a drop of water. We sucked the leaves off the olive trees, which helped a little. By the time it got dark, Chato had reconsidered. 'I don't know why I'm going over to the nationalists anyway; I'm a poor man. I have nothing; really, I should be with the reds.' I was furious. 'So why the fuck are you switching sides, then?' And he told me with that pathetic look in his eyes, 'I just want to be with you, Juanito.' There was nothing for it, so I warned him, 'For the love of God, Chato, don't you dare say you're a red once we're with the fascists or you'll get me shot. I wouldn't put it past you.'

"So we kept going, just picking our way through clumps of earth, and after a while he came up to me with his gun slung over his back and said, 'I'm going back to Andújar, 'cause I'm not on anybody's side. I need to go home.' He may not have had a house to go back to by that point, but his family did have a shack up in the mountains, where it was too dense even for the rabbits, much less reds or fascists. I said, 'Look, you're not going to Andújar. You won't make it past another olive tree alive, 'cause I'll shoot you first. I'll blow your fucking head off, Chato, so you just keep on walking.' And I fired a round

into the air, and that shut him up. It finally got dark and
we made our way for Porcuna, through the olive trees,
and Chato started up again. 'We should just head for the
Sierra Andújar, hide in the shack, and wait for the war to
end; no one'll find us there.' But I wouldn't hear of it. He
was so scared, he'd trip and stumble, like a baby taking his
first steps. We walked for a long time, and when day
broke, we headed up the slope toward the nationalist
trenches. On the way up, our guns slung over our backs,
we shouted, '*¡Arriba España!* Don't shoot! We've come to
join you! *Viva* the Falange!' Then they ordered us to
throw our guns over the barbed wire. So I threw mine,
but Chato was scared his might break, because at training
camp they'd forced us to treat our guns like our girlfriends. . . .

"Anyway, a few soldiers came out to help us through the
barbed wire and took us to a shack where two lieutenants
took our statements. I gave away every red position on the
map: barracks, kitchens, everything. Then, with the two
long-range cannons—Felipe and Leona—they shelled the
reds' positions at lunchtime. A few other deserters later
told us we were right on target with the kitchens—the
pots flew up in the air and the lentils made it all the way
to Regomello spring."

Castro and Estrella have reached the old mining company building, which now serves as the officers' lodgings.
The sentry at the door stands at attention; Estrella does
the same.

"Castro, are you tired?"

"Not really, Lieutenant."

"We skipped dinner. What do you say we go to La Tota's? They make good roasted potatoes. My treat."

La Tota's is an old shoring-wood depot that's been rented out by a Legion barmaid named Tota. The decor consists of thick cobwebs, ensigns, and regimental coats of arms. Sitting at a couple dozen tables—some round, some square, some of which are planks resting on sawhorses misappropriated from a bakery—are about fifty low-ranking military men: common soldiers, sergeants, sergeant majors, and a few young lieutenants and second lieutenants. An old Roma flamenco singer breaks into song. He's sitting on an improvised stage made of four barrels, accompanying himself on an old guitar. Soldiers, too, sing in unison, keeping time by banging their thick glasses against the tables.

As gents, the regulars are fine,
   they drink petrol like it's wine;
As gents, the regulars are boors,
   they'll fuck goats and they'll fuck whores

Castro and Estrella take a seat at an empty table near the singer's platform. They order a half liter of wine and two roasted potatoes each. The second lieutenant hardly touches his, so Castro eats all four with gusto. Estrella orders another half liter of wine and offers the singer a glass. He raises his glass in thanks.

"To your health, gentlemen."

The singer's old and gaunt body supports his shriveled face, aquiline nose, and limp gray mustache. The expression of resigned exhaustion on his face looks familiar to Castro.

"Hey, you're not from near Andújar, by chance, are you?"

"No, sir, from Granada, but I've been in Andújar a fair bit, shearing sheep."

"Ah! That's why I recognize you. Juan Castro the blacksmith is my uncle."

"Oh, sure! Great man, your uncle. He still alive?"

"He's in red territory, so who knows? We'll just see what's in store when this is all over and we go home."

The singer drinks in silence, pensive. "Damn *payos*," he says. "You Spaniards sure made a mess of everything."

After their third half liter, the second lieutenant orders a half bottle of cognac—the good stuff, not the rotgut the army plies soldiers with to fuel their aggression the night before a skirmish. Second Lieutenant Estrella, not practiced at holding his liquor, is quite drunk.

After a break, the singer breaks into song once more, this time with feeling:

I'd rather be dead and buried
Than spend my whole life here

Puerto de Santa María
Is torture and agony.
Where'll this little boat take me,
Crossing the peaceful sea?
Some say to Almería
Others say Cartagena it'll be

"We should get going, Lieutenant," Castro suggests.

"Call me Pepe, Castro. Listen, we're friends, aren't we?" the second lieutenant slurs.

Castro's a little drunk, too, but he's still lucid.

"Of course we are, sir, but I prefer calling you Lieutenant."

"Okay, call me whatever you want."

When they get up to go, Estrella insists on paying for everything.

"Don't they say a second lieutenant's first wages are for his uniform and his second for his funeral? Well, these are my second wages, and I want to spend them on my friend Castro; let the third go for the funeral."

He buys another half of cognac on the way out, just for good measure.

"For the road, Castro, in case we get thirsty. No good being thirsty."

Outside, the second lieutenant keeps drinking. He has to lean on his friend's shoulder to remain standing.

"You know, I really admire you," he says to the corporal.

"*You* admire *me*?" Castro's shocked. "The things you come out with, Lieutenant!"

"I do. I admire you because you had the balls to switch sides. I don't have the balls to do that."

"You don't have to, Lieutenant. You're already with the nationalists."

They've reached a dark alleyway. The second lieutenant downs the rest of the cognac in one go and then smashes the bottle against the wall.

"I mean I don't have the balls to go over to the reds!" he confesses, his voice hoarse. "That's where I ought to be, with my people, defending the republic!"

Castro thinks he might faint. He looks both ways. Could anyone have heard this incriminating confession? There are Military Information Service agents everywhere. What's this lunatic talking about? How could he make such a risky pronouncement to someone he hardly knows?

"Don't say that, Lieutenant; that's nothing to joke about."

The officer stops. He places his hands on Castro's shoulders to keep his balance, stares into his eyes with a sincere, penetrating, drunken stare, and says calmly and firmly, "I'm not joking, Castro. I've never been more serious in my life. But I had to get drunk to open up to you, because even though you might not know it, you're the only friend I have around here. I should have been out there fighting for the republic, but instead I'm here, feeling like a coward, scared shitless because I don't have the balls to go over to my side."

"Lieutenant, how can you say that? You, an educated man! You know how bad the republic is!"

"Bad? The republic? Oh, my friend. The republic has its problems, but it's so much better than the band of criminals and traitors who rose up against it just because they want to hold on to their privileges, the thieving bankers, the lazy aristocrats, the dishonorable militia... You don't know what freedom really is, because you were born in your exploiter's backyard. You're like a bird used to his cage. But let me tell you something, something you should never forget: Until you're really free, you're not a man. Don't forget it. And Franco and Queipo and the bishops, the only thing they're going to do if they win the war is chain the people down."

"Lieutenant, you're rambling, please be quiet; if anyone hears you, we'll be sunk."

The second lieutenant vomits onto the asphalt in the plaza. Castro helps him stumble to the fountain at the center, shoves his head beneath the spray of water, and splashes cold water onto his neck.

"Lieutenant, for the love of God, pull yourself together a little or this'll be the end of us both!"

The shock of the water helps the second lieutenant collect himself. Castro takes him to the officers' lodgings and, with some help from the reserve guard on duty, puts him to bed in a guard's cot. He throws a blanket over him.

"Don't worry," the reserve guard says, "this is the third drunk officer tonight. If they can't make it up the stairs, they sleep it off down here."

Castro goes back to the transit quarters.

"Well, this is a fine time! What do you think this is, a hotel?" Sergeant Major Peláez admonishes, half joking. He's on duty this week.

Castro can't get off to sleep for a while. The second lieutenant's revelations have left him troubled. Finally, overtaken by drowsiness, he turns over to join the chorus of snorers.

Chapter 13

The third company has been on a tour of duty for a month now, through frosts and heavy rains, soaked clothes, no firewood, and cold food. They've been in muddy, stinking trenches teeming with huge rats that scurry around, feasting on dead bodies. The icy north winds howl mercilessly through the guards' and scouts' posts, leaving their skin and lips cracked. They smear on wax, oil from sardine tins, and horse fat for boots, to no avail. Given the circumstances, shaving is sheer torture. Most men have grown several days' worth of beard, concealing lice and scabs on their faces. The second week of December they were shelled almost daily and infiltrated by enemy forces who came to test their lines, endangering their positions on Cerro Gamonal—between Cerro del Médico and Mano de Hierro—while leaving four men dead and a dozen wounded. The first company, in contrast, has lost only one man: a new recruit who lost his mind, stuck a Breda grenade in his mouth, and blew his head off.

Finally the reinforcements arrive so they can enjoy a few days at the rear, in Belmez. The soldiers clamber into trucks with an enthusiasm belying their weather-beaten faces, cracked lips, and bloodshot eyes covered with sties from having been scratched by filthy hands. Castro and the muleteers make the journey with their mules, this time carrying no load: The animals need a break too.

In Belmez, the soldiers shower and change their shirts and underwear. They're also forced to undergo a radical procedure aimed at improving their hygiene: They leave their clothes, blankets, and bedrolls on the mining-company shop floor, to be boiled in enormous cauldrons. A walk through the sanitary barracks is also compulsory: There, health workers will dust them with delousing powder. Pino refuses, insisting the powder decreases his libido and that, regardless, they'll be reinfested in a few days anyway.

"You're right about that," the health sergeant admits, "but you'll do it anyhow, or my name's not Braulio."

It takes a team of strapping health workers to break Pino down, while jibes and comments fly from his comrades.

Next they're led, naked, to showers that stink of bleach and disinfectant. Amid teasing and laughter, they continue down a narrow cement hallway lined with bronze showerheads that discharge high-pressure jets of water from both above their heads and below their knees.

"What the fuck is this, Sergeant?" Heliodoro asks.

"It's to clean your balls; they're full of crap."

The jets of hot water release a dense mist that's actually quite pleasant. Several health workers herd the lingerers along with reed canes.

Pino gets an erection and jokes with Aguado, who's walking ahead of him.

"Ramón! Oh, Ramoncito! Look what you've done to me! If you don't hurry up I'll catch you!"

"Don't come near me with that, pig. God knows how many times the doctor's treated you already, for it to get all swollen like that!"

"What doctor? This is my natural size, that's why the girls are so crazy for me; it's not like that pathetic little sausage you've got there."

Castro and the muleteers are assigned a big house comprised of spacious, airy rooms next to the best stables in town. They spend the first morning carting straw in from nearby hayricks. In the afternoon, they join the rest of the company to review their training. Sergeant Otero makes them learn the bugle calls: reveille, mess call, assembly, sick call, drill, adjutant's call, call to arms, attention, call to prayer, fall out, attack, fire, cease-fire, retreat, the general, tattoo, call to quarters, taps.

"Sergeant, what is it about the mess call that makes it prettier than the reveille?"

"What it is, is that you're a lazy pig, and all you think about is food."

Every afternoon the captain inspects the troops. Saturday they sound the reveille at three in the morning, and the men fall in with all their impedimenta for rifle inspection in the plaza.

"This is starting to look like Pancho Villa's army," Sergeant Otero admonishes. "You'll never make anything of yourselves. Tomorrow, when you fall in for Mass, I want your belts perfect: four clips per pouch, four pouches (two on each side of the buckle and two in back), eighty bullets total, and no empty pouches; I know some of you wise guys use them for your tobacco and lighters, but if I catch you, there'll be hell to pay. Fall out!"

During their time there, Castro makes up any excuse possible to go to Pueblonuevo and see Concha. One Sunday afternoon, after Mass, she introduces him to her parents, and he invites the whole family out for a vermouth at Bar Paraíso. Concha's mother appraises her potential son-in-law with an expert eye and inquires about his family. Castro doesn't contradict the information Concha has given them: His father is middle-class. He senses reservations—or perhaps distrust—in her mother's sharp glance. *That's only natural,* Castro thinks. He tries to calm his fears: No one can verify information about families in the red zone. He takes great pains to appear as elegant and confident as possible. How would Concha's mother react if she knew that when he returns to normal civilian life one day, it will be as a simple sharecropper and keeper of the marquis's estate, or that his mother is basically a servant who keeps his house? And what about Concha herself? How will she take it? Sometimes he wonders when he'll actually tell her the truth. His courtship began as a simple attempt to talk her into bed—without him realizing it, it has turned into something else entirely, something proper and official. If two lives are going to be joined together, as he hopes, then he should come clean, even if only bit by bit. But he can never seem to find the right time. He's thought about sending Chato, having him tell her the whole story, since he knows it and loves Castro's family. He pictures Chato building him up. "They're poor, but *very* honorable." But then he dismisses the possibility. As if Chato wouldn't fuck it up! "Well, Valentina, looks like we're just going to have to leave this one until the war's over. Best just to let things lie right now."

One Monday when Concha's accompanying her father to Córdoba, Castro goes to the station at seven-thirty to greet them during the train's brief stop. She emerges from the carriage into the train hallway and, during the fleeting moment they're alone together, gives him a quick peck on the lips. Before he can register his surprise, she pushes him back off the train; the conductor has just blown the whistle. Castro, from down on the platform, contemplates the mischievous smile Concha flashes him from the window. A kiss on the lips. The first one. Up until now she'd held out.

Castro is happy. He waits until the train disappears in the distance, trailing a plume of black smoke, then saunters back to his lodgings. The kitchen attendant serves him coffee and gives him half a can of condensed milk— it pays to have friends—and a thick crust of bread, split open and toasted, dripping with melted pig fat. After that hearty breakfast, he goes down to the stables and harnesses Valentina. It's the same routine he's seen his father perform countless times on market days.

"You'd never even think we're at war, eh, Valentina?"

Man and mule head out to the countryside, toward a hillock near the castle where good grass grows. Castro leaves Valentina to graze while enjoying his solitude, a rare commodity in the army.

The countryside is beautiful, even in winter. Castro imagines what it must be like in spring, after a rain, covered in rockrose and thyme.

"Valentina, this must be real pretty in spring, with the rockrose, and the lavender, and the rosemary in bloom, full of color."

Castro wonders sadly if he'll see it, if the war will be over by then, or if it'll last through another winter. Another winter? He harkens back to winters in Los

Escoriales, the cool smoke that smelled of branches when he lit a fire to make *migas*—fried bread crumbs—at dawn almost every day for don Federico and the hunters before they went out. He lets himself drift off into the compassionate haze of nostalgia.

When darkness approaches, Castro returns, stables Valentina, and joins his comrades in a tavern. Led by Aguado, they sing in unison:

> Oh, the regiment loves to drink wine
> And drink rum 'til our money's spent
> With women we have a good time
> Regiment, regiment, regiment

The night wears on and the singing finally stops. Half drunk, the men launch into philosophical discussions.

"We live like animals," Aguado speculates. "Misery is what brings us together here. Nothing unites people like misery. At war, we're tight as brothers—we could all get shot any minute and your men are all you have for consolation. But when the war's over and we go back to our lives, to our homes, you'll see, we won't even know each other anymore; we won't even *want* to know each other anymore. We'll walk right past each other and think, 'Look how poorly he's dressed,' or 'Get a load of his airs and graces.'"

"What are airs and graces?" Chato asks.

The others don't know either. They look at Aguado expectantly.

"Like when you try to pretend you're something you're not. Like when you think you're better," he declares.

"Ah."

"Well, I've never had airs and graces," Heliodoro exclaims.

"What makes you think you and me could have airs and graces, when we're the ones who're starving to death?" Pino replies. "You have to be at least a sergeant major to have airs and graces. Not just anybody can have them."

Chapter 14

Lieutenant, do you know what airs and graces are?"

Second Lieutenant Estrella looks at Castro suspiciously. He's managed to avoid him successfully for almost two weeks, but they've just bumped into each other. He's been worrying for days about the secret he confessed the night he was drunk. If Castro turns him over to the Military Information Service, as is his duty, he's a dead man. They'll court-martial him and he'll be sent to military prison, or the firing squad. He rehearses his defense, denying everything. After all, it would be his word against a corporal's. And then suddenly he realizes that a denial would negate the very essence of his republican faith, like Saint Peter before Christ, and he feels ashamed.

"Airs and graces? Well, like arrogance, like trying to seem like more than what you really are."

Castro's smile lights up his wide peasant face.

"Then that's what I have with my Concha: airs and graces. We've become engaged." Castro runs his hands through his hair. "You know what worries me, though, Lieutenant? Now that the war's almost over, I'll have to tell her I'm not the man she thinks I am, and I don't know how she'll take it. You know what women are like."

"Do you want me to write her another letter?" Estrella offers.

"Not this time, Lieutenant. I'm going to see her tomorrow night, and if I can get up the courage, I'm going to tell her the truth and we'll just see what happens. For now, I bought her a card I think she'll like."

Castro removes a small package from his jacket and shows the lieutenant.

Two lovers embrace on the card: a man with curly hair and a neatly trimmed mustache and a woman with a perm, wearing a carnation behind one ear. They're gazing adoringly at a bouquet of flowers. Across the bottom of the card reads the following verse:

With the warmth of each day
true love makes tender
the bud's bouquet
the flower's splendor

"Very pretty," the second lieutenant murmurs, his mind on another matter. "So, Castro. We had a good time the other night, eh? I sure did tie one on. Boy, was I drunk."

He wonders whether his sense of worry comes across to Castro.

"Lieutenant, you shouldn't drink so much; wine loosens people's tongues and then they talk nonsense. . . ."

"Well, I only talk nonsense to my real friends."

"If that's what you're worried about, have no fear; my lips are sealed," Castro reassures him, serious. "I feel very indebted to you."

"Indebted to me? Why? Because I wrote a few letters to your girlfriend for you?"

"Well, there's that, too, but mostly because of the zeppelin."

"The zeppelin?"

"That day we went from Peñarroya, remember? You explained how zeppelins fly. And that's enough for me to feel indebted to you for the rest of my days."

"That was no big deal, man!" Estrella protests.

"It's true, Lieutenant. Do you know what Master Federico, the marquis's son, said when I asked him? 'You just worry about plowing and don't waste your time staring up at the sky.' I asked some hunters at Los Escoriales, too, and they ignored me. And you know what? I'm starting to see that things aren't always as simple as ignorant folks like me think they are. A lot of stuff my friend Churri told me makes sense now. Course, he used to read

the marquis's books in secret, and I've never cracked a book in my life. It's like I'm allergic to the ink on the paper."

Castro and Second Lieutenant Estrella talk a little while longer. Castro tells him about the Marquis of Pineda's family, especially the marquise, Doña Lucía Val de la Giguera y Sácz. "A grand lady, really posh. Thought she already had one foot in heaven. At Christmastime, when me and my sisters were little, she'd call us all to the door of the big house at Los Escorialcs and give us each one silver *peseta*. We'd bow for her—wearing our best clothes, scrubbed clean—and thank her together." Castro tells him about the marquise's children, about don Federico, a good-for-nothing who thinks about nothing but cars and women—though he *does* know how to play tennis.

"Do you know what tennis is, Lieutenant?"

The second lieutenant nods.

"It seems there's nothing you don't know about, Lieutenant," Castro says. "The marquise's children, *Señorita* Virtudes, *Señorita* Cayetana, and *Señorita* Victoria, they're all gorgeous and they dress like princesses out of *Blanco y Negro* magazine. You can't imagine how good they smell, Lieutenant; they wear perfumes that take your breath away! Sometimes they come down to Los Escoriales for a vacation, 'cause they're normally in Madrid or Sevilla or Bia...Bia..."

"Biarritz?"

"That's the one, sir. And sometimes they bring their friends too. In the summer they go swimming in the pool by the tennis court, and when they return to Madrid, me and Churri go swimming in the very same water they swam in."

Castro doesn't mention the fact that they also used to masturbate, hidden among the fig trees by the wall, while spying on the daughters in their bathing suits—though Castro himself, out of respect for the family, looked only at Pilarín, *Señorita* Cayetana's friend who used to come down from Madrid to spend a few days in the mountains.

The next day at lunch, Cárdenas says to Castro, "Hey, Juan, one of the reds says he knows you. Some guy from your town."

"From my town? What's his name?"

"I don't remember; he said to say hello from Manolico from Pirricaña or something like that."

"You mean Manolico from *Pirriñaca?*"

"That's it, Pirriñaca."

"I know him! Yeah, he joined the militia. Good kid."

"Well, he said to tell you hello and that he's in the same battalion as Churri, who says hello too."

"Churri?" Castro asks, a lump forming in his throat.

Churri's alive. And he's out there, somewhere.

That afternoon, Castro goes out to water the animals. At the watering hole in Pilar del Llano, he orders Chato to take the animals back to the stable. Castro goes for a walk with Valentina.

He climbs a hill dotted with old holm oaks and some good grassland. Then he sits on a rock and holds back his tears. Churri's alive, and he's close by. He's been thinking about him for months—his best friend, though they fell out when he joined the militia. His father had said, "Juanito, you shouldn't be friends with Churri anymore: He's going around to all the taverns in town stirring up the workers. If word that you're friends with him gets back to the marquis, our entire family will suffer."

Churri had talked to Castro about politics, too, which led to several arguments.

And now he's out there somewhere, close by, and sends his greetings. Castro is so glad he's alive.

Valentina is munching some green shrubs, perhaps more out of courtesy than hunger, since Castro always makes sure she has plenty of barley. She approaches Castro and shoves her muzzle into his back, asking to be scratched.

"*Ay*, Valentina, life's tough," he says, scratching her big hard head, the little clump of hair and flesh between her ears, the soft whiskers beneath her chin, her long, muscular neck.

Night descends swiftly in the winter. The cloudy sky is just a faint violet glow breaking through the invisible horizon.

"Let's head on back, Valentina."

In the muleteers' kitchen, a fire is burning; the green

wood gives off too much smoke, but it warms them. The mule drivers are roasting the chorizos sent to them by a girl who writes Aguado. They're passing the wineskin too.

"This is the life," Heliodoro boasts, leaning to one side to let out a fart.

"I've had better myself," Pino replies, letting out another without bothering to raise his bottom from the bench.

"Well, so have I, dammit!" Cárdenas adds. "And so has *he,* and him too—but this is what we got, Pino, so make the best of it."

They pass the wineskin once more.

"You're awful mopey tonight," Amor says to Castro.

Castro shrugs.

"Here come some good chorizos," Petardo announces, pulling the spit off the fire. "Hold out your bread, boys!"

The soldiers extend their ripped-open crusts, and Petardo deposits a chorizo sausage into each one. The men fold over their bread, squeezing the sandwiches tight so that the grease seeps out, soaking and softening the bread.

"You know what they call this up north?" Aguado asks. "Pregnant buns."

"Well, pregnant buns are goddamn delicious," Heliodoro replies with his mouth full.

They eat their sandwiches in silence.

"I'm going to take a piss," Cárdenas announces.

"Spanish cocks piss in flocks," Castro responds, getting up to accompany him.

He's been waiting for an excuse to speak to him alone.

They walk outside and piss in silence, aiming high, in routine competition to see whose stream goes farther.

"Hey, Eladio, about what you were saying about Churri, that guy from my hometown, I was thinking...I'd like to see him. To ask about my family, more than anything. You know where I'd find him?"

"The men from the second company go down to the well at the hermitage every other day. That's where they meet up with the guys from the other side. You have to go unarmed. You wouldn't believe all the wheeling and dealing they do: tobacco, cigarette papers, hash, chocolate. That swap meet the Moors have going is nothing compared to this! If you want, I'll go with you. I've been a couple of times."

"When's the next one?"

"Tomorrow afternoon."

The next day, after the customary inspection of positions, once the officers have gone back to their huts, Castro and Cárdenas wander down to the second-company sector. A dozen soldiers and one sergeant are waiting at an advance post that's been blown apart by a mortar shell.

"How's it going, Castro?" the sergeant greets him. "You going to the market too?"

"I am, Sergeant. I may be able to gather some news about my family from a guy who's from my town."

"I tell you, Corporal"—the sergeant looks away—"I really couldn't give a shit about your personal life. Everybody ready?" He raises his voice. "Yeah? Let's go, then; I want this orderly, no racket, eh?"

They file out through one of the holes in the barbed-wire fence, and, as they pass the scout's post, the sergeant gives the man on duty instructions.

"When we come back it's going to be near dark, so I'll flash my light three times. Got it?"

"Yes, sir, Sergeant."

On the way, they're joined by half a dozen Moors wearing *jellabas* and carrying bedrolls on their backs; they'd been waiting in a hollow. Half a mile later, they reach the stone wall that surrounds the hermitage of the Virgin of Antigua—patron saint of Hinojosa—which has been spared in the war. There they take the right fork in the path that leads to the Arroyo well, where a group of militiamen are gathered. The nationalist sergeant quickly greets his republican counterpart. Those who know each other from previous trips say hello, huddle together, take their merchandise from their haversacks, and start dealing. The reds are flush with cigarette papers, since the Alcoy factory is in their territory, but they have no tobacco. The nationalists have no paper but—with the meadows of Granada and the Canary Islands under their jurisdiction—plenty of tobacco. They're smokers before fighters.

Castro recognizes Manolico from Pirriñaca: cross-eyed, potbellied, laughing as usual, despite three years at war.

"How's it going, Manuel?" he calls.

"What, we're not going to hug, two brothers like us?" the militiaman says, holding out his arms.

They embrace.

"I'm glad you're okay."

"Same here."

Manuel wipes away a tear.

"There's a friend of yours over there," he says, nodding toward the well. "He came to see you. You remember Churri?"

"How could I forget?"

Churri, tall and dark, is sitting on the parapet. He seems thin, possibly the effect of the blue boilersuit he's wearing under his leather jacket. He smiles openly at his old friend.

"Juanillo, how you doing?"

After hesitating for a moment, the two men fall into a long, silent hug. Castro can't hold back his tears. He wipes them away with the back of his hand, smiling in embarrassment.

"Damn, Churri, look at me, crying like a baby!"

Churri slaps him on the back and stuffs several packets of cigarette papers into his friend's jacket pocket.

"Oh, Benito, I didn't bring you any tobacco! We were in such a rush," he apologizes.

"You think I care?"

"You don't know how happy I was yesterday when I heard you were alive. This damn war . . ."

"I was glad to hear about you too. I thought: *Look at little Juanillo, good to see that bum with his mules, even if they are fascists.* That was always your thing, so good for you."

"How can the mules be fascists!" Castro protests, laughing. "They're not reds or fascists; they're smarter than all of us."

Churri smiles. He stops solemnly to think for a moment, and says, "You know, all this time it's bugged me, how bad we left off, you and me. We were like brothers— more than brothers. You don't know how much I think about you, how much I wanted the war to end so I could just find you and make up...."

Castro squeezes his friend's arm.

"Well, now we have, Benito. I thought a lot about it, too, our falling out. It's my fault, you know. I was just worried about the rumors. My father didn't want me to take a stand with any anarchists."

"Come on, man! It's both our fault. I was pretty stubborn myself. I should have told my section commissioner to go to hell when he asked me what I was doing with a fascist friend."

"Forget it, Benito. Water under the bridge. You still like chocolate?"

"That goes without saying, Juanillo!"

Castro takes out half a chocolate bar and splits it with his friend.

"You remember the chocolate the marquis gave me?"

"Swiss. How could I forget?"

They eat in silence, sharing a crust of bread Churri pulls from his pocket.

After a while, Castro broaches the question he's waited to ask Churri. "So, tell me about Andújar. How's my family?"

Churri's voice darkens. "Your father's still in jail in Jaén. They were going to free him, but when you joined the fascists, they extended his sentence. I think he's making straw baskets that your mother and sisters sell to get by. There are two anarchist co-ops in the marquis's houses now—the ones in La Quintería—but they're not doing too well. It's hard, with the war and all.... Anyway, your mother and sisters have joined the co-op, so they have a share. They go with the rest of the women to pick garbanzos. Last time I had leave, I went to see Jacinta and bought a basket from her. I don't think she recognized me in my uniform. You wouldn't believe how she's grown! A real little lady now. But she needed new shoes pretty bad; you can tell they're not doing well, Juan. I tried to give her ten *pesetas* so she could buy some sandals, but she ran away. Maybe she thought I was looking for something else."

"Little Jacinta?"

"Almost everyone back home is having a real hard time. The war's taken a big toll."

Castro fingers the pocket of his jacket. "Look, Benito, I really hate to ask you this, but would you take them a letter from me?"

Churri hesitates.

"I can't do that, Juanillo," he replies gravely. "You know

that. How can I carry a letter from a fascist? But I can tell them I've seen you and that you're okay."

"Please. At least give them some money if you can; I'll pay you back when this is all over."

Churri nods solemnly.

"I'll try to give them a hand, if they let me."

They fall silent and watch the wheeling and dealing going on around them, soldiers from both sides exchanging merchandise and news. No one would guess they're enemies; no one would guess that tomorrow they'll kill one another if they can.

"Come. Let's have a smoke," Castro suggests jovially. "You probably need some tobacco, right?"

"And I bet you have no cigarette papers!" Churri replies amiably.

They laugh. Churri takes out his papers, Castro his tobacco pouch. They remain silent as each concentrates on rolling a cigarette.

"Well, all in good time!" Castro says. "The war will end sooner or later, and then we'll all just have to get along if we want to smoke. You think when this is all over everyone will be friends again?"

Castro flicks his flint lighter and holds it to his friend's cigarette, then his own. He takes a deep drag.

"Depends who wins," Churri replies, serious again. "If the republic wins, maybe; but if the fascists win, us poor folks are in for it. They won't shoot everyone, 'cause they'll need someone to work the land. But something tells me it's going to be hard times for us."

"Well, everyone has to pay for their crimes."

"Crimes?" Churri's angry now. "What crimes are those, Juanillo? The generals and the fascist gentry who rose up in arms are the criminals; all *we're* doing is fighting for a crust of bread, fighting for our children, for mine and for yours, even if you're helping the fascists, because they— your kids, I mean, the ones you'll have one day—they're not to blame. Maybe one day you'll open your eyes and see that."

"*Me?* What do *I* have to do with it?"

"You have everything to do with it, because you and me are slaves. Don't you see that? Did you know that kids used to be bought and sold, included with the price of land like olive trees? That's still happening, and it's not right. The republic tried to change that, with agrarian reform."

"Agrarian reform is nothing short of taking the land from its rightful owners. It's the same as a band of gypsies bedding down in your house just because they don't have one."

"It's *not* the same, Juan. Agrarian reform means that if a man works the land, cultivates it so it benefits society, then it should benefit him too. It means that good, arable land that could provide bread for the poor shouldn't be used as a hunting reserve or a stable for horses instead."

"Yeah? And where does that happen?"

"Right here, Juanillo, right here in Spain, on the very land you're standing on, but since you've never left La Quintería and never read a book in your life, or a newspaper, or anything, you have no idea."

"The Russians have you brainwashed with all that revolution of the poor; you don't know how wrong you are."

"It's not about Russia, Juan! We're talking about Spain, about our home. We're talking about the fact that children live like animals, and it's wrong. Compare the marquis's palace to your parents' house. You don't even have windows to view the countryside—"

"We've never gone hungry with the marquis, not a single day."

"Maybe *you* haven't, but others have. They've kept you content with a few crusts of stale bread, but . . . do you remember that day at Los Escoriales when we went into the big house?"

"Course I do."

"Remember how you couldn't take a single step without bumping into expensive furniture, silver trays, figurines, all those little trinkets from all over the world? And remember the rows of shotguns in the gun cabinets? Remember the rows of tiger heads, lion heads, six-point bucks, lined up on the wall? Remember the rugs in the hall, the way your feet just sank into them? You think it's right that some people live like that while others don't have enough to buy medicine? And what about that library with thousands of books, gold-leaf books that no one ever read?"

"*You* read some of them."

"I did, and that's why I'm telling you this, because you're a dimwit who refuses to educate himself. I've been reading everything I could get my hands on ever since I was a kid; I opened my eyes and saw the world for what it was."

"Or maybe all that reading led you astray. Me, I'm on the side of order, honest work, and peace."

"The side of *order*? What order is that? The order to kill, the order of the cemeteries? Can't you see? A few military *cabrones* rose up against the lawful government, and they managed to fool all the damn bumpkins like you. Do you really think it makes a lick of sense for the poor to fight to defend *them*?"

"I don't fight; I'm a muleteer."

"So what? You're still helping your exploiters! You have less sense than the mules you drive."

"You expect me to help the people who put my father in jail instead?"

"Dammit, Juanillo, your father's in jail because he sided with the fascists, because he kept kissing the marquis's damn hand."

"The hand that fed us."

"Look, Juan: A lot of stupid things happened at the start of the war; there were a lot of wrong turns, I know."

"You mean like burning churches? Killing priests and landowners?"

"Only a few out-of-control elements. It was wrong, it went against the spirit of the republic. But the law is in force now, and there are no more popular tribunals. Everyone here is trying to help win the war and bring liberty and justice back to Spain."

"You really think you're going to win the war when all you've done is lose one town after another?"

"You actually believe what Queipo says on the radio?"

"Do you expect me to believe what the reds say?"

An uncomfortable silence descends, erecting a wall between the two friends. They smoke without looking at each other. Then Churri pats his friend's thigh and says calmly, "You know what's wrong with this country? Ignorance. We're a bunch of illiterates, and good honest people like you are so ignorant they don't realize that their whole lives, and their parents' lives, and their grandparents' lives, have been lived in injustice; for thousands of years they've been exploited by priests and kings. And until people learn, until you take off your blindfolds, we're all in trouble."

"And when's that going to happen?"

"One day. The same things used to happen in other places and now they don't. The French revolted two hundred years ago; the Russians twenty years ago; why can't we too?"

The sergeants, who've been chatting on either side of a boundary line, now get up and shake hands, bringing the exchange to a close. Each returns to his men.

"Okay, time to pack up and head out."

Castro and Churri shake hands. Churri lingers, not letting go for a moment.

"The republic's done for," he confesses, "because the people who should be defending it are betraying it. Your generals are fascists: Franco, Yagüe, all those crooks who lost the war against a few ragged Moors in Africa. Now they want to profit off the blood of the people. But our side has no balls, they're a bunch of dandies."

"How can they be dandies if they're reds?"

"Reds? Ha! There aren't nearly as many reds as you think. Look: Casado is old line; Ibarrola and Escobar are a couple of holier-than-thou bastards who protect the priests; Matallana and Moriones are marquises; and Buiza is a dandy from Sevilla. They might have fooled some people, but they don't fool me. They'll all betray the republic. They say the war's lost, but all they want to do is surrender to the fascists."

"You mean, you *know* the war's lost?" Castro asks.

"Of course I know it, Juanillo! How could I not?"

"Then why don't you give yourself up? Come with me now, and I'll vouch for you, tell them you're a good man."

"I can't surrender. Don't think I haven't thought about it. But I remember that story about the beaver, and I just can't do it."

"What's a beaver, Churri?"

"It's an animal, like a rabbit but bigger. See, there was this beaver trying to escape from a hunter, but he couldn't.

He knew he was going to be shot, so he decided to cut off his balls, which is what the hunter was after."

"What? His balls? Holy shit!" Castro laughs doubtfully. "What'd he want his balls for?"

"I think they contain some expensive substance, some liquid they use to make perfume. Plus, the soft skin is used to line the buttons on cardinals' cassocks."

"Come on!"

"It's true! Anyway, never mind, that doesn't matter. What matters is that when the beaver cut his balls off, he died; he bled to death."

"So what the hell is that supposed to mean?"

"It means you can't give up your freedom even to save your life. Because without freedom, life's not worth living. And that's why I can't let myself be taken, because I'd rather be killed."

Castro looks pensive and then slowly shakes his head.

"Churri, you're too much. You think so much that you're going to die for your ideas. My grandmother, poor woman, she was right. She used to say ideas were the worst thing in the world. My mother warned me too. 'Don't you go following Benito,' she'd say. 'He's full of ideas.'"

"People are who they are, Juanillo. You're a slave; that's your calling. Your whole life you've been a slave to capital, and now you're a slave to Franco. You're the master's dog. And when Franco wins the war, you'll go back and slave away from sunup to sundown, and you'll be satisfied with the few scraps he tosses you. That's what you were born to do; it hurts me to say it, but it's true."

"You used to say the same thing back in El Higerón, in La Quintería. You think I don't remember? But you have your ideas and I have mine. You're not going to change my mind and I'm not going to change yours."

The republican sergeant approaches and interrupts them, telling Churri, "Comrade, we've got to go; it's getting dark."

Churri stands.

"Well, Juanillo. Still friends?"

They hesitate, uncertain whether to shake hands or hug. In the end they hug, clasping each other tightly.

"Juanillo, I don't know if we'll see each other again, but I want you to know that what's done is done. It's water under the bridge, and I'm your friend no matter what."

"Me too, Churri. I hope the war ends soon and we can go celebrate back in La Quintería with a nice calf and a wineskin full of wine."

Churri smiles sadly and nods.

They take their respective paths without turning around. Churri trails behind his men slowly. Castro's men have started back, too, and only a few Moors remain, packing the smoking papers they've traded into a gas-mask case. Castro sees a man with one foot, recognizes him as Mohammed.

"Corporal mule driver met your friend, eh?"

"Yeah. He's from my hometown."

"Good to have friends."

The Moors take their path and Castro takes his, alone and pensive. In the cold moonlight, the patches of bramble cast eerie shadows.

"Know what I think, Valentina? As far as you and me are concerned, they can all go fuck themselves. You and me, we just want to get out of here alive and get back to La Quintería, 'cause there's going to be a lot of work to do when we get there."

But now he has a new concern. He turns back to look at the hill where he imagines Churri must be walking, but all he can see is the vast darkness of the night.

Chapter 15

December 17, 1938. Third Triumphal Year. Castro finagles a leave to Córdoba for horseshoes and nails. A company driver takes him to the station in Belmez. The quartermaster's freight train departs at six-thirty, but Castro instead buys a ticket for the eight o'clock, which Concha and her mother will be riding. They're going to Córdoba to buy checkered fabric for tablecloths and napkins.

Castro has just received word that Lieutenant Estrella has been shot in the leg. He's convalescing in Fuenteagria and won't be able to write any more letters to Concha. Castro greets the two women with a bright smile. Now he's on his own.

Doña Concha has already complained about the train's

lack of hygiene and comfort. "We used to only travel first class. Of course, back then we had a first-rate hotel; it was known internationally! Anyway, let's pray the war ends soon so things get back to how they should be."

Concha and Castro sit opposite each other on benches by the window, exchanging amused, complicit glances. Concha is wearing her blue dress, with a matching jacket secured with giant buttons, and a touch of makeup. She looks beautiful, and Castro is waiting for his future mother-in-law to go out into the hall so he can tell her so, so he can stroke her hand, at the very least.

The train stops at two unmanned stations along the way and then again in the middle of nowhere, due to engine trouble. While they're repairing it, people get off to look for coal on the tracks and wild asparagus in the fields. A passenger who's traveling with a goat lets it graze while they wait. Finally the train is fixed. A whistle informs the passengers, who rush back in raucous jubilation, anxious not to be left behind. They resume their journey, and finally the train pulls in to Córdoba at around noon.

"We're in a rush," Doña Concha says. "Where do you need to go, son?"

"To buy horseshoes and nails."

"We have more than that to take care of. Why don't we meet at two o'clock in Plaza Caballo to have *calamares* at La Malagueña? It's very reputable."

"That's a great idea, *señora*."

As they walk off, Castro in one direction and the women in another, Conchi says to her mother, "We should treat him. After all he spent on the earrings and the suit fabric he gave me, I don't think he has much money left."

"Don't be ridiculous, child!" Doña Concha replies sternly. "You can't be a pushover! After all, you're engaged, aren't you?" Conchi nods quickly. "Well, then! He has to chip in. If you don't show him what you're worth now, he won't appreciate you once you're married. Besides, if he's as rich as he says he is—which I don't believe for a second; he's got *farm boy* written all over him—then he'll know a gentleman always pays. And don't forget that even if we're struggling right now because of the war, we *are* ladies: always have been, always will be."

"Yes, Mother."

After a platter of *calamares,* three beers, and three bananas for dessert—totaling forty-three *pesetas*—Doña Concha suggests they go to the Palace Theater in Victoria Gardens, to watch a Rudolph Valentino movie, *The Son of the Sheik.* Castro buys the tickets—seven *pesetas* and fifty *céntimos*—and watches the movie sitting in the third seat: Conchi is in the first and her mother in the second, between them. Two or three times they manage to exchange rapturous glances. Oh, how he longs to hold Conchita's hand! In the darkened theater, Doña Concha's head cuts through the projector's beam of light, highlighting a downy mustache he's never noticed before, since she apparently bleaches it. *Will my Conchita look like that in a few years?* he wonders uneasily.

On the way back to Peñarroya, Castro spends his last three *pesetas* on a half dozen *magdalena* cakes he buys off a vendor in the station.

Despite the presence of Doña Concha and the financial setbacks, it's been a wonderful day, far from the war and the trenches, with Concha looking so pretty.

The next day, a new guest arrives at Pensión Patria: Alfredo Piña Coscuyuela, a sergeant major from the infantry, who's joining the Second Transmission Battalion to lay telephone wire between the Sierra Trapera and Sierra Mesegara positions and the Extremaduran Army Corps. At breakfast, the officer commends the high-quality olive oil on his toast.

"Really marvelous oil. Is it local?"

"Yes, sir," the hotelkeeper replies. "Do you know much about olive oil?"

"A fair bit," the officer replies. "Before the war, if you'll forgive my immodesty, I was the biggest oil broker in Andújar."

"Andújar, you say?" The hotelkeeper seems surprised. "We have a good friend from there! I don't know if you know him: Juan Castro Pérez; he's from a very well-off family. They've even got horses."

"Juan Castro?" The officer looks pensive. "Hmm. Doesn't ring a bell."

"Well, actually he's from La Quintería, right next to Andújar. His parents have a big farm in the mountains, in Los Escoriales."

"That's the Marquis of Pineda's hunting preserve," the officer clarifies. "Oh, I know! Juan Castro must be the marquis's servant, the boy they have in charge of the horses and other livestock; he's the caretakers' son."

"Servant?" Bartolomé Rama repeats, making no effort to hide his disappointment.

"Yes, he's a servant. Good family. As I said, his parents are the caretakers. They call his father Birdie, because his grandfather was a loon and he raised birds."

"Well, he acts like a real aristocrat."

"He does?" The officer laughs. "I guess Birdie's son is a peacock!"

Bartolomé Rama couldn't run to tell his wife fast enough.

Chapter 16

So, the very same day we went over to the nationalists, they took us to Bujalance and then to Castro del Río,
where they interrogated us all over again. The day after, we
went to the recovery center, which was in the Good Pastor
school in Córdoba. There were at least forty of us—some
who'd switched sides and some still undecided, since back
then just about anybody taken prisoner said they were
switching sides. Every day they took us to the Civil Guard
barracks and made us dig antiaircraft shelters.

"I didn't know anyone in Córdoba, but I remembered
that don Federico once brought some friends from there
to Los Escoriales, very rich people. So I informed the lieutenant in charge of the workers' unit, and he sent me and

two Civil Guards to the Farmworkers' Club to find anyone who might vouch for me. The secretary called a few
members and managed to get hold of a wealthy warehouse
owner. So we went to his house—more like a palace, with
a gigantic courtyard and a marble fountain, swarming
with maids. He came out with one of his sons—a tall
skinny kid, with lieutenant's stars—and I recognized him.
'Do you remember me, sir?' He stared at me sternly and
shook his head. 'Sure you do, don José, remember? A few
years back you came to El Lugar Nuevo, near Los
Escoriales, to go hunting, and I took you out and brought
back the partridges you shot.' Finally he remembered.
'Oh! The zeppelin kid!' You have no idea how happy I was
he remembered. 'Yes, sir! The one who asked about the
zeppelin.' He laughed and said to his father, 'You wouldn't
believe how much this kid pestered me about the damn
zeppelin!'

"So in the end he told them I was the Marquis of
Pineda's servant, the caretakers' son, and said, 'Four or five
years ago, he seemed like a good kid from a law-abiding
family; now, I can't vouch for anything he's done since
then. So see if the marquis will; he's in Biarritz.'

"That, I didn't like so much. But at least they could see
I came from a right-wing family, a family that served the
Marquis of Pineda. Luckily, after a few days I found a dis-
tant relative, a farmhand named Moya who'd moved to
Fernán-Núñez. Since he didn't have a telephone, one of
the club members who lived nearby offered to tell him a

relative was in Córdoba. The next day, Moya turned up and vouched for me and Chato both. That was real lucky, 'cause anyone who didn't have references ended up in a concentration camp.

"After seven or eight days the Civil Guard called us up to join a fortification company in Villafranca de Córdoba. And that was the end of our civilian life; from then on we were back in the military. They gave us secondhand uniforms—dirty ones—and a pick and shovel each.

"There were forty or fifty soldiers in the fortification company, and they took us all to dig trenches every single day, over by Villa del Río. Hard, thankless work. And that's where me and a guy from Campillo de Arenas made a pact and said we weren't doing it anymore. Guns, maybe, but no more shovels.

"Chato refused to join us; he kept working. He reasoned that if we refused to work, they might shoot us. He begged us not to mess around with these guys.

"So me and the guy from Campillo spent a few days doing nothing, until the lieutenant came and told us we'd better get back to work or we'd get him in real hot water. Still, we were miserable in the sappers company, so after a few days we ran away to a recruiting office in Priego and enlisted in the Legion. But the next day, a sappers squad showed up to take us back. On the return trip to Villafranca, the captain, don Manuel Díaz Criado, called us into his office and said, 'So you're deserters, eh? You think you're better than the rest of us? Is that it? You think

I like being in charge of a sappers company, digging holes all day like worms, when I've been an officer in the Legion my whole life? Believe me, it pisses me off more than you, but I just bite the bullet, so you can fucking quit whining and do the same!'

"In the end there were no arrests, because don Manuel, who was from Marmolejo, knew the Marquis of Pineda and he remembered my father. And that's what saved us.

"We spent a month or so in Villafranca, and the truth is, except for the pick and shovel, it wasn't really that bad. It was quiet on the front, there was no shelling, and when the soldiers' wives came, they'd sponsor dances that lasted all night, with accordions and everything. Then they took us to Lopera and gave us guns; that was probably in July, when we started guard duty and armed service. It wasn't too bad. Not much action in the trenches, a few shots fired, maybe a few mortar rounds, but shortly before we got there it had been bad—lots of men killed. Then both sides calmed down again, and all they'd do was talk shit over the loudspeaker at night. So a national would brag, 'Red Roger! We had potato stew with ox meat for dinner tonight! How were your lentils?' The reds would get mad. 'If you weren't such bastards, you wouldn't take it up the ass so much, you Franco-loving fuckers!' 'And if *you* weren't such *Pasionaria*-loving commie sons of bitches, you might know who your fathers were; only reason I don't curse your father is because it might be me!' They'd go on and on.

"The companies would alternate weeks in the trenches and in town, changing guard on Sundays after Mass and after lunch, which they served in the plaza in front of the castle. The reds knew that; that's when they'd start up with the artillery fire; it never failed. The priest—a round man from the Levante—would scrunch himself up like a turtle, his head all the way down in his cassock, when he heard the shells whistle. You could tell he didn't put much faith in Providence. He said Mass in about five minutes; he'd even skip the consecration. Then, after him, the next one we got was a chaplain from the Legion; a real wino. When he raised the chalice for the consecration, he'd tap around with his toe like he was at a bar trying to rest his foot on the rail.

"Anyway, even though things were relatively quiet on the front despite a few shots every now and then, you had to be on the lookout all the time, just in case. After a few days, I knew everybody there and got myself a job as assistant to Lieutenant Cejudo; he was from a good family in Córdoba. The lieutenant had a girlfriend back home, and every day he'd send me to the post office to deliver his telegrams for her. But before I went to the post office, I'd take them to this girl in town who was in love with him. Her name was Fina Martínez; she was from a wealthy family and she'd give me something to eat in exchange for my services.

"Fina and her sisters—there were three of them—had a grand piano in their living room, and since they had nothing to do all day, she'd just play, or embroider, or make bobbin lace or bandages for the hospital. I remember one of the verses they used to sing from '*La Madelón.*' Fina would play along on the piano.

Oh, how I love to see you, airplane
I know you're bringing freedom my way
I want to fly with you forever
And embrace Franco and his men!

"In Lopera there was this one sergeant major, good person but real dumb, and I used to play jokes on him all the time. One day, he'd had too much wine and said, 'When we free Jaén, that's when we'll see if Castro's a red or not.' I laughed but I didn't say anything, and then a few nights later he said to me, 'Castro, let's check out the scouts' posts.' So I grabbed my piece and a clip with five bullets and we went outside the barbed-wire compound. We were checking out the scouts between enemy lines, and when we were down in a little gully hidden from the parapets, I stood back for a minute and I said, 'Officer, how can you trust me if I might be a red?' That scared him stiff; you could just about hear his knees knocking. I walked ahead of him so he wouldn't be scared of getting shot in the back, but it was too late. He didn't relax until we returned to the trenches.

"I had no news of my family and I couldn't write to them. Some prisoners from Andújar told me my father had been arrested on the farm, tied up with a rope, and taken from there to Jaén. This guy Raimundo who arrested him—he was a good guy, but when the war started he turned communist, and the reds were nasty. They'd send the tough guys to the undecided citizens, to threaten them; that's why they sent Raimundo to see my father."

"We stayed in Lopera a few months, until they dissolved the company and sent us to boot camp in Utrera, where they trained companies and battalions. After two or three weeks they'd send them out to the front. Me and Chato tried to hang back with the dimwits, the clumsy ones who couldn't catch on, so we managed to stay at least three months, but then the captain called a few of us up and said, 'That's it! I've had it with you morons! You're going on maneuvers, *to* the front, and *at* the front. And if you can't buck up, may God strike you down!'

"I'd put down on my file that I was a master blacksmith, even though I couldn't pound a nail into the wall. But I'd learned a thing or two watching my uncle in La Quintería shoe horses. So they sent me and Chato to the Peñarroya front, and I met a lieutenant I knew from Lopera. He was desperate for the girl from the smoke shop, who happened to be a friend of mine. She put a word in for me, and they ended up taking me on as master blacksmith and corporal muleteer in the Third Battalion of the Canaries Falange, because the blacksmith they had at the time was an old drunk who neglected his duties. I asked the captain if Chato could come with me as an assistant, and they put him down as muleteer too.

"I didn't know what I was doing, so I ended up maiming the first couple of mules I shod, but no one said anything about it because even the veterinarians were students; they knew even less about the animals than me. I just took the nails out, took their shoes off, and eventually they healed. I had to treat a few animals too. That was a little easier, because my father had taught me to disinfect wounds by making a paste out of vinegar and bran. Bran's what's left over from wheat, the stuff you grind up really fine to give the chickens. You just baste it on the animal's oozing wound, and it clears up."

Chapter 17

¡Viva Christ the King!

Pueblonuveo, December 19, 1938
Third Triumphal Year

Juan,

I've thought alot about what I'm going to say in this letter and wondered if it would be better to tell you face to face but in the end I decided to write because I'll be able to say it better this way and besides that way my feelings and my spite wont get in the way.

Let me assure you I'm perfectly calm as I write this. I spent a long time in the chapel thinking it all through.

I've cried alot of tears since I found out youve been deceving me, but I promised myself that I wouldn't cry over you or any man ever again. I'm considering my vocation very seriously. As you know, before I met you I wanted to become a nun, and after this great disappointment I think that maybe God put you in my path on purpose. Father Próculo always says God talks to us straight even if the path that leads us to Him is crooked, and you've given me the push I needed to get back on the road to Him and to leave behind the world and it's deceets.

I'm not a selfish women and I think rich and poor alike are all God's children and what really matters is honor and having a pure heart. I was taught Christian values and that we should all help our fellow man and we're all God's children. So you can imagine how surprised I was to learn that you've been lying to us all all this time, that ever since you very first spoke to me at the dance the only thing out of your mouth has been lies. A very trustworthy, Falangist Christian has thankfully seen fit to fill us in on your background and tell us how your the marquis's caretakers son and you've never been anything but a mule driver all your life. That's a dignified profession and I don't know why your ashamed of it, but you just kept on talking about horses and hunting and hobnobbing with the marquises and it turns out the only reason you were even with them is because you were on the hunt as there servant, carrying there rifles and serving them food. It was all a lie because you thought I wouldn't find out anyway since you were planning to leave me as soon as the war was over, right?

The thing I'm most sorry about isn't that I was foolish enough to believe you, though I'm sorry about that too, but at least that suffering I can offer up to God in my religious vocation. The thing that hurts me most is how you treated my parents, who took you in like a son and who didn't deserve to be disrespected like that. They did nothing wrong, though my mother could tell the second she laid eyes on you, she said Conchita, daughter, he's not the man he makes himself out to be, he's got farmboy written all over him. She said, he's not what he says he is, and me, like a fool, I was so blind I even quarreled with her about it.

All I ask you now is that you send back my photo, letters, and the lock of hair that you have. If your a decent man, a man of your word, you'll do it. Put it all in an envelope addressed to me and send it with someone who's coming to town, because I never want to see you again. If you have any respect for me at all, don't come here or try to see me, I beg you. I'm sending your letters back with this one since I also found out that you can't hardly write and Second Lieutenant Estrella was writ-

ing your letters for you and finding out all of my personal feelings which explains why he used to look like he was laughing whenever he saw me, the swine. I'm also returning the earrings.

    Please don't try to come see me. You have nothing to explain. I swore before the Virgin that it's all over between us.

                      María de la Concepción Rama Anula

¡Viva España! Franco, Franco, Franco!
José Antonio Primo de Rivera. Present!

Chapter 18

An hour before dawn the alert to ready arms circulates; they're awaiting a red offensive. Rumors have been circulating about the attack for days, but no one actually believed them; after the Battle of Ebro and the liberation of Cataluña, it was supposed to be all over for the reds. Surely they couldn't muster enough spirit to attack now, could they? For months, more and more soldiers have been defecting to the nationalists, and they're all telling the same sorry tales: Their lentils are full of weevils; they have no blankets, no medicine; and if they can't wangle themselves a pair of boots, they have to make do with the rope-soled shoes the quartermaster corps supplies them with.

Bitter-cold wind slices like a knife through every crack in the hut; it shoots under their tabards, through to their skin, and down into their bones. The muleteers shiver, huddled around a half barrel riddled with holes and filled with burning sticks and twigs. The smoke from the green wood stings their eyes. They smoke in silence, resigned, sitting on empty munitions crates, their feet up on bricks and flat stones to keep them out of the mud. Aguado has managed to get hold of a fine-tooth comb, a nitpick. He runs it slowly through his beard and hair, collecting little white dots—lice eggs—which he throws into the fire.

Suddenly they hear a far-off sound, a pop.

"Looks like it's going to heat up," Heliodoro says.

Hearing the whistle of the shell grow louder as it approaches, they listen, holding their breath, until it explodes.

"That hit the second company," Pino says matter-of-factly.

"Don't worry; they're not going to leave us out, you'll see," Petardo replies.

More cannon fire, first intermittent and then almost constant: two, three, five, nine... They can't distinguish individual sounds, so are unable to work out the shells' trajectories. All the howling blends together. The earth trembles. A quick succession of explosions rattles the area, so close that chunks of the earthen roof fly off.

"Oh, shit, oh, shit! This is it!" Castro shouts. "The second it lets up, take the mules to the hospital and get ready for Commander Soler's orders!"

He prepares to leave.

"Where the fuck are you going, with all this shit flying everywhere?" Cárdenas asks, alarmed.

Castro pauses a minute before responding. "To get Valentina. I left her grazing in the field by the well last night."

"Jesus, Juan, what were you thinking? At least let me go with you," Chato offers.

"No, you stay here, I'll be right back. It's not far."

He emerges from the hut and disappears in a cloud of dust and smoke that leaves the pale dawn light tinged with tawny hues. Castro makes his way through the twists and turns of the trenches.

"He's *obsessed* with that mule!" Amor says. "I mean, at first she was skinny, at death's door, so fine, help her. But now she's the fattest of them all! Shit, he loves her more than his own girlfriend!" Castro has failed to share the contents of Concha's last letter.

"Yeah, well, to each his own," Chato replies solemnly.

No one else says a word. They're all thinking the same thing: How could they die now, when the war's about to end?

Castro knows the quickest way to the meadow that borders the ravine, just beyond the first platoon's trenches. He treks through the ditch that leads from the trenches to the outpost. The sudden whizzing of a shell forces him to the ground, hands covering his face, eyes closed, mouth open. He counts to ten, slowly. When there's no explosion—

must be a defective shell—Castro gets up and continues on his way. He's worried Valentina, spooked, might have wandered behind enemy lines, like when he first found her. Valentinilla! The mule is the only thing he's going to get out of this war, which he couldn't care less about. He's grown fond of her, can't stop imagining her in La Quintería, can't stop picturing his discharge, his arrival home in uniform, looking thin, his mother and sisters rushing out to greet him, tears in their eyes, while his father, who sits smoking in the doorway, sees the mule and says proudly, "She sure is going to be a help to us, son."

The force of a blast near his body hurls him into a ditch and buries him under an avalanche of dirt. He gets up, trembling, wipes the mud from his face, brushes dirt off his chest, and keeps walking, out in the open field now. At least he knows no one will come out of the shelters during the barrage; no recruit's going to stick his nose out and shoot him, mistaking him for a Red Roger. But coming back with Valentina after it eases up is going to be tough: The troops will be at the parapets, fingers on the trigger, tense and ready to attack, with a fifth of cognac in their veins. *I'll have to wave my white handkerchief and take Valentina through the second platoon, where they all know me,* thinks Castro as he reaches the grassy clearing where he left Valentina hobbled. She's gone.

"Valentina!" he shouts. "Where are you, baby? All hell's about to break loose! Valentina!"

He heads into the bushes and finds her broken hobble behind a thicket.

Shit! Oh, shit, shit, shit. That stupid mule's taken off!

Castro heads into no-man's-land, toward enemy lines. Meanwhile, the attack has started to die down. Maybe the reds were just using up their ammo, never the attack anyone believed it might be. Good.

He skirts a low hill, takes a worn trail, and spots the ruins of a small farmhouse in the distance. He searches it, to no avail. A riverbed runs down behind the house, and at the far end there's a cluster of eucalyptus trees. Perhaps Valentina's gone all the way off down there. Without thinking, he treks farther and farther. A flight of republican *Natachas* zooms overhead.

This is it, this is it! The reds are attacking and the dumb mule's gone!

He's totally exposed in the open field, and that's not good. Gathering his courage, Castro traverses the clearing. Every step he takes brings him closer to enemy lines, and the damn mule is nowhere to be found.

She's not hiding in the eucalyptus trees either, but some more ruins appear farther on: a shack with a fig tree by the door, and an arbor with vines creeping across the ground at will, having strangled the rotted wood that once held them up. Castro searches the area as the *Natachas* fly back over again, higher now, and faster, having unloaded their deadly cargo. He can hear the sounds of battle to the left, to the right, everywhere. Shells fly, whizzing and howling in every direction. The thundering of explosions has become a constant, evil drumbeat banged out by a thousand hands, all out of time.

"What the fuck!" Castro shouts, terrified. "I'm right in the middle! Where the fuck are you, baby girl?"

He continues on toward the reds' lines. Finally, just beyond an oak grove, Castro sees Valentina standing, still and serious, ears back, muscles tensed, clearly spooked. He approaches.

"Easy, now! Easy there, pretty girl!"

The mule watches his approach and makes no attempt to run; in fact, she lets her head drop as if waiting to be petted.

"Oh, I see! Now you're sorry, eh? You have no idea how worried I was," he scolds affectionately, scratching her forelock, between her ears.

The animal stands complacently and nudges him, rubbing her enormous head against his body.

"Okay now, Valentinilla, no time to waste. We've got no business being here, and things are really heating up."

He puts on the mule's halter, then leads her by the rope. Mule follows muleteer tamely. Castro retraces his steps but, before reaching the *cortijo,* stops short. The corporal cocks his head and listens closely, thinking he heard a sound that wasn't coming from the sky, thinking it was close and right there on the ground.

He pricks up his ears.

That was it. That sound. A drone you can never forget, even if you've only ever heard it once. Tanks.

He listens hard, hoping he's imagining things.

"For the love of God, those are tanks, and they're getting closer!"

He yanks on Valentina's halter and picks up the pace. It's a red offensive, with tanks, and he's caught in the middle of it all, just leading a mule along. He could ride her, even bareback. They could trot, even gallop, but then they'd be more obvious still. The reds might think they were cavalry and open fire. Better to look like a simple mule driver trying to save his mule.

"This has nothing to do with us, Valentina. We gotta get out of this mess."

A sound to the left startles him. The squat young man dives into the undergrowth. But there was no bang, no explosion. Castro stops short behind some tall bushes, but they don't hide him completely.

A hundred feet away, a republican tank appears, sheets of steel and chains clanging, its cannon aiming ominously. "Did they see us?" Castro, in a panic, yanks Valentina off to the right, where the undergrowth is thicker. He's fully aware of his compromising situation: The reds' advance parties are here, and he's alone, far from nationalist lines.

"*Ay*, Valentina, this looks bad. If they catch me, I'm dead. I'll be shot for being a traitor; I used to be on their side!"

The mule trots, following the corporal. They duck behind a crag, which shelters them for a second. They take a narrow path down to the riverbed, where there's a partially concealed trail leading to the nationalist lines. Castro takes it and, trotting down a gentle slope, runs straight into a republican tank. Too late to hide. If he tries, the gunner will mow him down. He stops and puts his hand up.

"I surrender!"

The steel monster advances toward him. Castro, standing before his mule, watches it approach. He wonders if it will just run him down and thinks about the mess of crushed bone and torn flesh a tank leaves in its tracks.

The metal beast stops a few feet in front of them. A steel latch is unbolted. From the top hatch of the armorplated turret comes a hand, then an arm, and finally the top half of the commander's body. He's wearing a padded black leather cap, some type of helmet.

"Do you mind telling me what the fuck you're doing here, Juanillo?"

Beneath the leather cap, Castro recognizes Churri's familiar features.

"Christ, Benito, it's you? In a tank?"

Churri smiles.

"Commander of a T-26: best tank in the world! Sorry I couldn't tell you the other day; military secret. But shit, Juan, what the hell are you doing out in the middle of all this?"

"Well, first I lost my mule, and then I got lost myself."

The lower hatch screeches open, and another head wearing an identical black leather cap pops out.

"I got the fascist right in my sights, Lieutenant. Want me to open fire?"

"What the fuck are you talking about? Don't you dare open fire!" Churri shouts. "This is a friend of mine. Get your ass back in that tank right now, and don't let me see your face again."

The gunner shrugs, obedient, and closes the hatch.

"Now what?" Castro asks.

"Now you get the hell out of here and let me through. We're really sticking it to the fascists, so you better try to escape. Won't be easy with that mule, though; the two of you together stand out."

"Oh, man, thanks, Benito..."

"Shit, Juan, don't thank me. Just get the hell out of here! Good luck!" Churri raps on the tank's turret forcefully and shouts his order down inside the hull. "Okay, kid, let's move!"

The tank skirts around Castro, then continues on its way amid the clamor of grinding metal and connecting rods. A thick plume of black smoke billows up from the exhaust pipe. The engine splutters once or twice, clanging loudly.

"Oh, man, you have no idea how lucky we were, baby girl!" Castro strokes Valentina's neck. "We might as well have been born today, 'cause any other day we'd be dead, that's for sure."

It's only then that he realizes his legs are trembling so

badly he can hardly stand. He drops Valentina's lead rope and sits down in the shelter of a palm tree. A humid north wind is blowing. After a while, a gentle rain begins to fall. Off in the distance, between the short breaks of cannon fire, he can hear the hollow sound of hand grenades exploding. The republican troops are launching an attack on the Sierra Patuda trenches. He can hear artillery fire on Cerro del Médico too. Castro can't make his mind up. *To get back to my lines, I have to go through the heart of it; but if I stay here, I'll get caught. They'll shoot me the second they find out I'm a traitor; not even Saint Peter himself could save me.* He decides it's better to risk returning and remembers a section by the Cruz pass with such rough terrain that there aren't even any trenches, just a lookout post. Might be easier to get back that way. "When I reach La Toleda's house, I'll take the Pocitas path and come out at El Rector. If the reds haven't occupied it, that is."

He picks up Valentina's lead rope again and heads into the densest part of the thicket, where no one will see them. Another encounter might not have such a happy ending. A short while later his fears are realized: Two armed militiamen cut him off. One trains his submachine gun on him.

"You! Where you going with that mule?"

Castro drops the rope yet again and raises his hands. "This time we're fucked, Valentina."

"Eh! Get over here, boys!" The one with the submachine gun signals to his men.

Out of the brush come more militiamen, carrying long, pointy Russian bayonets and rifles.

"What's your name?" the one with sergeant's stripes on his cuffs and cap asks.

"Castro."

"What are you doing here?"

"I just came out to find my mule; she got lost."

"You with the Falange?"

"Me? No way! I'm a worker," Castro lies, though not entirely. "I just got caught on the wrong side, but I'm from Jaén. Before the war I was with the National Workers' Federation."

"Unbelievable. Fascists always turn out to be lefties the second they get caught! Look, I don't know if you're on the left or the right, and I don't care." He smirks at his comrades. "All we want is for you to take us prisoner."

Another militiaman approaches. "Juanillo, good to see you again."

Castro recognizes Manolico from Pirriñaca's squint from beneath the steel helmet, which he's wearing with about as much poise as he'd wear a chamber pot.

"Manolico? What're you doing here?" Castro asks.

"Just trying to get taken prisoner, see if we can make it out of the war alive. Can you do it?"

"Take you prisoner? I ... I don't quite get it."

"Christ, prisoner! Yes!" the sergeant shouts. "Let's get a move on; we want to make it to a concentration camp before they bump us off."

"What do you want *me* for? I don't have anything to do with it!"

"Aren't you a corporal?"

"Yes."

"With the nationalists?"

Castro shrugs. "I guess, yeah..."

"So take us prisoner, dammit!"

"But I'm not even *armed*!"

"What are you talking about, not armed? Here, I'll give you my tommy gun, you say you killed a red and took it off him, and then you take us prisoner. You come off like a hero, and we don't get our heads blown off the second we cross the fascist lines. So hurry the fuck up and take it so we can get going; they're on our tails."

The sergeant hands Castro his submachine gun. The corporal accepts it with a trembling hand. "I'm not sure this is such a good idea."

"Really, I couldn't fucking care less."

Manolico looks toward the sergeant. "Hey, what do we do with *our* poppers, Cosme?"

"Get rid of your bayonets, take off the bolts, and put them all in a sidepack."

The soldiers obey.

"Now sling them in your shoulder bags, butts up, to show you're laying down arms."

The sergeant hands Castro the heavy sidepack full of bolts.

"There. Now you've disarmed us! Take us to the fascist

lines, to a platoon where they know you. And if we meet an advance party on the way, you shout out so they don't shoot and you tell them you've taken some reds prisoner."

Castro, carrying the submachine gun, follows the group of republican prisoners, Valentina trailing behind. "*Ay,* Valentinilla, look at all the shit you put me through just by breaking your hobble."

Meanwhile, the Battle of Peñarroya, the last battle of the Spanish Civil War, rages on. Forces from the Forty-seventh, Thirty-first, and Sixty-eighth Divisions of the Republican Army's Extremaduran Army Corps have broken the nationalist front in both the Valsequillo and Granja de Torrehermosa sectors and are advancing rapidly, their tanks preceding them. The republicans are crushing all resistance and manage to open a five-kilometer breach in the nationalist lines, between Cerro del Médico and the Sierra Trapera and Sierra Mesegara.

Chapter 19

Pablo Benavides—wearing striped pajamas, a cape thrown over his shoulders, service cap pulled right down to his eyes—uses his elbow to wipe the misty window of his room and looks out. He hasn't slept a wink, what with the tractors towing cannons, cars driving by, trucks full of soldiers, ambulances, horns honking, orders being shouted; it's been going on all night. When day breaks, Plaza Peñarroya becomes a seething mass of men and military equipment. Beneath his window passes a canvas-covered truck with half a dozen mud-covered bare feet and one sergeant's arm—judging by the stripes on the cuff—sticking out the back. Another load of bodies, still warm, off to the cemetery.

"What a shithole," Benavides mutters. "Valley of

Pedroches, my ass. Valley of *Cojones,* more like it. The bastards don't fire a shot the whole damn war, and then the second I show up all hell breaks loose. And everything was going so well in Sevilla!"

But Sevilla is a long way away, and the national edition of ABC newspaper has sent him to do a feature on life in the trenches. He blew into town on January 5, after lunching in Córdoba with a lady friend, and took a room at the best *pensión* he could find, the Imperial. Then, just as he was getting ready to report from some nice, peaceful trenches, the shit hit the fan.

Benavides dresses quickly to go to headquarters, where one of the commanders, a family friend, will make travel arrangements to get him back to Córdoba. He doesn't care if it's by train, car, or truck—even if he has to ride with the cargo. He just wants to get out of this dump as soon as possible.

He's hardly walked a hundred yards when a wing of low-flying red bombers appears and panic breaks out. Benavides trembles just thinking about it: A bomb goes off a mere hundred yards behind him, knocking down a house he's just passed. Benavides hurls himself to the ground, terrified, though in his article he'll say it was the force of the blast that knocked him down and will go on to describe it—with elegant metaphor—as the deadly flick of an invisible giant's hand. When the reddish cloud of brick and adobe dust settles like a thick fog, Benavides sees the rubble of two houses.

"*Ay,* Mother of God, Blessed Virgin, if you get me out of this I swear I'll give up my whoring and gambling and all my unsavory habits!"

As he's closing his temporary deal with divinity, he takes refuge in the doorway of an old granite house that appears solid and reassuring. From there he continues praying and promising.

The planes make two more passes, machine-gunning vehicles in the plaza, then fly off. The journalist stays in his little shelter until he hears people shouting orders and engines back on the street. Only then does he venture from his hiding place.

"Is it over?" he asks a liaison passing by.

"Seems so."

Benavides is carrying his Agfa camera, a gift from his friend Captain Kluger of the Condor Legion. This, he realizes, is an excellent opportunity for his article: here on the front line, in the heart of it all, bullets flying, surrounded by danger. First he'll photograph the newly demolished homes. He sits on a step to rewind the film. Then suddenly he feels it. A soft, warm trickle dripping down his thigh.

"I'm wounded!" he cries joyously. "I've been wounded! It's a battle wound!"

He pictures the headlines, his face gracing the front page, wearing his field jacket with the collar upturned, sporting a dreamy Clark Gable look. *Pablo Benavides, our fearless correspondent, wounded on the combat front.*

He goes back inside the house and, behind the door,

takes off his belt, unbuttons his fly, and pulls down his trousers. The stench assaults his sensitive nostrils before he has time to see the mess. It's true: He shit his pants. But it's not his fault, it's his sphincter's, that traitorous little muscle that has a physiologically involuntary reaction, tending to relax in the moments of greatest stress, like when a bomb drops right behind your head.

"Fuck, fuck, fuck!" Benavides says to himself. "What the hell am I supposed to do now?"

Luckily, the damage has been contained to his underwear. Benavides shuts the door all the way—Lord knows he wouldn't want anyone sneaking up on him in this compromising position—and removes his trousers and underwear with the utmost care, so as not to spread the trouble. He'll have to ditch his underwear, which is a real shame because he'd put on his best pair in case he managed to have his way with a nurse. He leaves them more or less folded in one corner of the hallway. Then he scavenges some papers and old rags from the next room and uses them to wipe himself as best he can, finally putting his trousers back on and returning to the *pensión* to perform emergency ablutions and get a new pair of underpants.

After that accident, Benavides feels like a new man. A correspondent baptized by fire; he is nothing like those ninnies holed up in Sevilla typing away with one finger, never having left the paper's office. Not him, boy. He's right here in the midst of it, center stage, where it's all going down, balls of steel. He spends all morning roaming from one place to another, taking notes and snapping photos. At the command post, the colonel who'd been pleasant to him the night before orders him to stay out of the way and not take any pictures. He spends the rest of the day trying to find a way back to Sevilla and waiting for a call he put through the switchboard to the paper. Finally they tell him he's got a line, and the editor at the newspaper on the other end orders him to stay and write a feature extolling the nationalist forces.

"Yes, sir!"

"Listen, Benavides."

"Yes?"

"It can't be defeatist, understand? At a time like this, we have to raise spirits and reassure everyone that victory is ours. I want a story to boost our readers' morale, to let them know we've won."

"That's easy for you to say. It's not safe here. How am I supposed to write an optimistic article when the nationalists switched sides as soon as they saw the republican tanks and lost six towns in one offensive?"

"I'm sure you'll figure something out."

Back at the *pensión,* Benavides stares at the wood-fire stove, which has died down to a few embers. He decides to return to headquarters and see if he can rustle up any good news: a counterattack, an enemy aircraft shot down, anything.

A man of action, Benavides makes heroic decisions. On the front, a war correspondent has to be as weather-beaten as the troops. Starting tomorrow, he'll no longer shave. He strides down the middle of the street, disdaining the sidewalk, mud up to his ankles. In the plaza the bodies of four Falangists are strung up, with signs on their chests reading, *Thief.*

"What's all this?" he asks a soldier.

"They were caught robbing the houses of families who fled to Córdoba after the bombing."

Benavides looks away. He rushes by and heads for the command post. The colonel has purple bags under his eyes that grow larger by the minute.

"It's a difficult situation, but we've got it contained and that's all I can say. Now, please don't bother me anymore."

He turns his back to tend to a liaison who's brought him a report.

High-ranking officers come and go without giving Benavides a second glance. There's nothing he can do. He's just getting ready to leave when, passing an open door, he overhears something promising.

"Go see Colonel Valiñas and ask him if they've interrogated the prisoners that mule driver brought in."

A mule driver took prisoners. Sounds optimistic.

"Yes, sir, Commander," the orderly replies, heading off to carry out his order.

Benavides accosts the soldier in the hallway.

"Excuse me, son. I'm a journalist from ABC." He flashes

his newspaper identification with photo. "What's this I hear about a mule driver who took some prisoners?"

"Yeah, a muleteer, one of the guys who transports munitions and *nicanoras*."

"Tell me about it," the reporter urges.

The soldier glances at the office door apprehensively. "Look, if the commander comes out and sees me talking to you, I'm dead."

Benavides pulls out a box of Camels. "American cigarettes! Hard to come by," he says, tucking the packet into the soldier's top jacket pocket.

The soldier smiles graciously as he pats his top pocket.

"Where could we go talk for a minute?" prods Benavides.

The orderly takes him to a small inner courtyard piled high with empty boxes and crates.

"So, tell me what happened with this muleteer and the prisoners!"

"Not much to tell, really. A muleteer ended up behind enemy lines in the confusion of the initial push. He showed up this morning with nine reds he'd taken prisoner. That's all I know."

"Daredevil!" Benavides comments. "Look, son. This is the story I've been waiting for: a shining act of heroism to make everyone forget the setbacks of the war."

"I have to go," the orderly says. "If they see me messing around, I'll catch hell."

"One last thing," Benavides says as the orderly walks away. "Where can I find this muleteer?"

The orderly stops and takes a cigarette out of his jacket pocket. He points to a bench.

"Wait there; I'll be right back."

He disappears into the building and returns a minute later.

"His name's Juan Castro Pérez, and he's in the third company of the Third Battalion of the Canaries Falange, the one defending Cerro del Médico."

"But isn't that where all the action is?"

"Yes, sir."

Benavides finds the idea of going to interview the muleteer on the front, in the midst of battle, unsatisfactory. He's had enough, after this morning's debacle.

"If you're lucky, you'll find him in the quartermaster's depot. The reds blew most of our trucks to pieces, so almost every company has to get their munitions and reinforcements by mule now."

Benavides walks out to the plaza and asks where the quartermaster's depot is. Someone tells him it's in the old movie theater, on the next street over, behind the church.

The street is overflowing with automobiles, carts, and mule trains. A sergeant major is screaming his head off, trying to impose some sort of order, brandishing a formidable club he's using to hit cars, animals, and people alike. A dozen soldiers, blanket capes tucked into their belts, are loading a truck with wooden ammo crates by the rope handles. In the office—visible through the window of the old ticket booth—a fat, ruddy sergeant is in such demand that he doesn't know who to attend to first. Benavides shows him his press credentials.

"General Queipo de Llano sent me. I'm looking for Corporal Juan Castro, head of the Third Battalion of the Canaries mule train. Anyone here know him?"

The sergeant asks the other clerks.

"Any of you know Juan Castro, Canaries Third?"

"He was here not half an hour ago to take a load of munitions," one replies.

"And where do you think he is now?"

"Back at the front, my guess. Don't think he'll be dawdling today, with this mess."

Juan Castro is not, in fact, back at the front. Two blocks away, he's gathered up the courage to go see Concha, who receives him in the entryway, cold and distant.

"I told you I want nothing more to do with you! Do you mind telling me why you came?"

"Please, let me explain—"

"I don't need any explanations. I don't want you to tell me any more lies; I've had enough," she replies, her eyes flashing with anger and spite.

"But, Concha," Castro begs. "If you're talking about my feelings for you—"

"I'm talking about the fact that you had me believing something false. Do you think I was only after a rich man? Is that what you think of me? All I want is a sincere, honorable man who loves me, and you made out you were a gentleman . . . with your shotgun and your partridges. Turns out you're a muleteer!"

"Being a muleteer is no disgrace!" Castro says defensively.

"You're right—lying is! *That's* the disgrace!" Concha replies, wiping away a tear with a handkerchief she had tucked into her sleeve, before slamming the door in his face.

Second Lieutenant Estrella would know exactly what to do right now; Castro has never lamented his absence so much. Unsure of what to say, he is about to knock again when a man wearing an elegant army jacket with an upturned leather collar accosts him.

"Juan Castro?"

Castro's eyes dart, looking for his rank; he must be at least a commander. But he can't see any stars. No military insignia at all.

"I'm a journalist." He introduces himself. "My name is Pablo Benavides, reporter for ABC. I'm looking for Juan Castro. I was told you might be him."

"At your service," Castro responds, unconvinced.

Benavides shakes his hand with manly vigor.

"Thank God I found you! I almost went back to the front before someone told me you hadn't yet left. I need to speak to you. It's urgent."

"Speak to *me*?"

"You took nine reds prisoner yesterday, didn't you?" Benavides says with admiration.

"Well, I didn't exactly take them. It was more like they surrendered, really."

"How's that?" He takes out his pen and reporter's notebook.

"Well, I was with my mule, leading her back after she'd gotten lost, and suddenly they just came out of nowhere and gave me their weapons. They wanted to come over to the nationalists and they saw their chance, with all the ruckus, so I took them, and when we got to the nationalist lines, they came over. I knew one of them, he's from Andújar—I used to tend pigs with him."

"*What?* You knew one of the enemies?" Benavides asks, scratching his head. "What a coincidence. And you recognized each other?"

"Sure, we'd just met up at the well a week ago."

"What well? What are you talking about?"

"The well by the Antigua hermitage. That's where we meet up to talk and barter."

"You telling me that you fraternize with the enemy?"

"That I frat...what?"

"That you get along with the enemy."

Castro goes on the defensive. "Look, I don't want any trouble."

He makes as if to leave, but Benavides grabs hold of his sleeve.

"I'm not going to get you into any trouble, I just didn't know that sort of thing went on."

"Yeah, well, it does, all the time, when we're not fighting."

Benavides thinks for a minute. He's not going to let anodyne reality get in the way of a good story.

"What you did was a heroic feat!"

"Come on. No, it wasn't. If they'd been looking for trouble, I'd be dead, but all they wanted was to surrender and get out of the line of fire. See, the Red Rogers are having a tough go of it, and they'd rather be in prisoners' camp."

"Sounds awful."

"At least there's no fighting there."

Benavides inhales the morning air forcefully and smiles.

"Let me tell you something in all honesty." He overcomes his disgust for Castro's greasy army jacket and throws an arm over his shoulder, buddylike. "It's not in your interest to say that. You're a nationalist soldier, and you can't spoil a victory. Did you know the reds broke our front lines and took six towns, and in spite of the reinforcements we still haven't managed to contain them? Well, that means that at troubled times like this we need heroic feats, and if you'll take my advice, you can be a hero, receive honors, medals . . ."

"Listen, I'm not interested in medals. All I want is for the war to end so I can go home."

"Where are you from?"

"La Quintería, near Andújar."

"Great place! That's where a page of the glorious history of our Crusade was written: the siege on the Virgin of Cabeza shrine!"

"Yeah, I know."

"How can it be that a man from such a heroic land doesn't want to contribute to the nationalist cause?"

"I am contributing; I'm a muleteer."

"Yes, but your modesty prevents you from becoming more. I'll make you a hero! Have you thought about the women who'll fall at your feet, offer themselves to you, legs spread wide open? Do you have a girlfriend?"

"Not anymore. She just slammed the door in my face 'cause she found out I'm poor, and the second lieutenant who used to write her letters for me just got shot in the leg and now he's been evacuated."

"You see? There's nothing wrong with being poor, but women like money, they like attention. If you can't give her one, give her the other, and you'll see how fast you get her back. Let her know you're a hero!"

"I said no! I tell you, I don't want any more trouble!"

Benavides tries everything to convince him, but the muleteer is more stubborn than his mules. There's no way.

"All right, at least let me take a picture of you."

Reluctantly, Castro poses for the photo. "Is this going to go in the paper?"

"That's the idea."

"Well, don't use my name. I don't want anybody to know, 'cause my whole family is on the other side. I wouldn't want to cause them any trouble. They went through enough when I came over to the nationalists."

"Oh! You mean you were with the reds?"

"Yes, sir. I'm from Jaén, so I got called up. But I came over here as fast as I could."

Benavides shakes his head. He's seeing Castro with new eyes now.

"A hero against his will! That's a shame; you've given me a lot to work with here, and I could put together an excellent story! Let me take one more photo. Here, out in the street so the light hits you."

Castro poses in the middle of the street.

The reporter shakes his hand and says good-bye. He takes a few steps and then turns around.

"Oh, I almost forgot. Who's your company commander?"

"Don Braulio Soler Mediavilla. He's from Galicia; before the war he was a captain in the Civil Guard."

Benavides scribbles all this down in his little reporter's notebook. He puts his camera back in its case and shakes Castro's hand once more.

"Good-bye, Corporal."

Castro watches him walk away, looking like he just stepped out of a magazine, in his boots and well-cut trousers, his jacket with the leather collar. He was wearing cologne too. He must be loaded. Then he looks up, one last time, at Pensión Patria. He's unaware of the fact that Concha is watching him through a crack in the shutters from the second floor. Castro approaches the closed door, intending to knock, but he stops himself, his hand in midair.

"Better leave it for another day, when she's calmed down a little. Maybe I should talk to Pepi first."

Concha watches him walk off, with his bowlegged muleteer's gait. "I don't know how I ever even fixed my eyes on him, with his boorish ways," she chides herself.

Chapter 20

Commander Soler's head is bandaged. During the January 5 attack, a stone ricocheted off a gravestone and hit him. It's nothing serious; being forced to retreat with only one boot—the other got stuck in the mud—in the face of the reds' advance hurt more.

Liaisons ferrying orders dash in and out of the command post, housed in a tiny *cortijo* behind Cerro del Médico. Engineers have just installed telephone lines, and not a moment too soon for Soler. "The positions at Cerro del Médico and Mano de Hierro are holding up, Colonel, but we lost a lot of men in the Antigua hermitage advance parties," he says into the line. "I sent out a replacement company, with a platoon of machine gunners. But basically, we're short on rifle ammo and hand grenades, especially if they keep up the offensive."

Castro wonders if he hasn't picked the best time to show up, but there's nothing to be done for it. When the commander hangs up, he stands at attention and salutes energetically.

"At your service, Commander, sir!"

The commander eyeballs Castro.

"What I see before me is a short man with a boorish face—the antithesis of a military hero." He snatches an open newspaper off the table and shows it to the soldier. "But have you seen the paper, Castro?"

The article on the center pages is circled in red pencil. Castro sees a picture of himself standing in Plaza Peñarroya, a blurry group of soldiers waiting for their lunch in the background. He opens his eyes wide.

"What you told that reporter is not what you told your officers, Corporal," the commander observes.

Castro goes on guard immediately. He can see it coming, maybe an arrest. *Why the fuck did I ever trust a reporter?* he wonders. *Maybe I'm as dumb as Churri says.*

"Commander," he says defensively, "all I told that guy was the truth."

"So you didn't disarm any reds, didn't take a whole platoon prisoner all by yourself?"

"No, sir, Commander. Is that what it says in the paper?"

"That's what it says," the commander corroborates with the hint of a smile that Castro doesn't quite know how to interpret. Could be good, could be bad.

"Commander, sir, I promise you that—"

"Do you know how to read?"

"Yes, sir, Commander," Castro responds, head high and chest out.

"Well then, take that paper and go read the article. Come back when you're finished."

Castro exits the farmhouse and sits on a stone ledge beneath the weak winter sun. He looks at his photo again, centered on the page: He looks like a somebody, with his blanket cape, his cap tilted to one side, his knapsack. He wonders if Concha's seen him. She must have; they get the paper at the *pensión*. Behind Castro in the photo, a group of soldiers stand lined up, waiting at the mess truck. The caption below the photo reads, **Peñarroya's hero of the day. Corporal Muleteer Juan Castro poses before the militiamen he took prisoner during the failed January 5 Marxist attack. In the truck, some of the supplies and munitions requisitioned from the enemy.**

"Jesus Christ, that guy has some balls!" Castro exclaims, amazed at the reporter's distortion of reality.

Next he reads the headlines: **A SPANISH HERO: MULETEER CASTRO,** and then in smaller print, **A modest muleteer captures ten fully armed Marxist elements during combat at Peñarroya.**

And below that, **Report by our correspondent on the battlefront, Pablo Benavides. Always on the news trail.**

Castro starts reading:

In three years of war, we've seen a lot of heroes in the Glorious National Army, but none so humble and modest as the man we proudly present today. His name: Juan Castro Pérez, one of hundreds of thousands of anonymous soldiers who risk everything in the trenches, even if it means writing the pages of their heroic story from heaven.

A simple peasant from a little village near Andújar—in the province next to Jaén, currently in the clutches of Marxism and awaiting its imminent liberation—this man has the mettle of his heroic predecessors, the martyrs who locked themselves into the shrine of Santa María de la Cabeza and wrote some of the most glorious pages of Spain's epic history in their own blood. This man, Juan Castro, initially drafted into the Marxist army by a simple fate of geography, knew that his rightful place was in the nationalist ranks fighting the communists, risking his life in the name of his homeland— so despite life-threatening consequences, he crossed over to our ranks.

Here, he was welcomed into the generous heart of Spain, and he requested the honor of fighting on the front line. That's what he's done for two years, serving in the line of fire, shining bright in every battle in which he has had the honor of fighting, bringing supplies, machine guns, mortars, and munitions to the most battered outposts, the most dangerous positions, then loading wounded and deceased nationalist heroes onto makeshift stretchers to take them back home. On January 5 of this Triumphal Year, this exemplary soldier was stationed in an advance position on the Peñarroya front when the red hydra, in their final death throes, made one final pathetic attempt against the stronghold comprised of the Glorious National Army's best men. Amid a torrent of lead and shrapnel, Corporal Castro realized that one of the mules in his charge had by chance wandered into a meadow pounded by enemy fire. Without giving it a second thought, he went off to find her. With no regard for danger, his only concern was to reinstate the long-suffering quadruped into national service. In the whirlwind of artillery fire, he realized that the mule, spooked by the proximity of the explosions, had fled from her safe pasture toward the territory still controlled by

Marxist rabble. What to do? A search for her could lead to his imprisonment or even his own death. But abandoning her would allow the mule to fall into enemy hands. Under those circumstances, Corporal Castro didn't think twice: He grabbed a weapon and headed into no-man's-land, the moment the reds were advancing under the illusory pretense that they could break nationalist lines. Suddenly, our hero spied his mule grazing beside a Soviet tank, behind which ten fierce-looking militiamen, armed to the teeth, were taking cover. Corporal Castro felt the ancient valor of the race who once conquered the earth coursing through his veins. As such, he prepared to enter combat without stopping to consider his diminished force against a large and well-equipped enemy. Approaching the reds, he aimed his rifle and ordered them to surrender. The ferocious emissaries of the Anti-Spain, seeing the cold-blooded courage of the hero who loomed before them in his five feet five inches of heroic manhood, felt their legs give way and dropped their weapons. Their leader was brandishing a late-model Russian submachine gun, which Corporal Castro quickly relieved him of. Then, pointing the gun at the group, he ordered them to set out for nationalist lines, leading his mule behind him. And so it was that a single man—a humble muleteer and his beast of burden—arrived at the national army positions when the reds' attack had been heroically repulsed, leaving the fields strewn with the dead bodies of these godless vermin. When we submitted this special report a day later, still hot on the news trail, these parasites with no homeland were still taking up their dead and burying them in the villages of the rear guard, where life goes on as it used to.

This reporter had the privilege of finding himself in the line of fire while hunting the news, during the apex of the Marxist attack. On the parapet of an advance position, bullets flying in every direction, sprayed by shrapnel from explosions of every caliber, your faithful correspondent saw this hero—a modern-day Crusader—advance unperturbed, immune to danger. Defying death, we came out to meet him, to embrace him, and to ask him the questions demanded by professional journalism. He's a simple man, content to have been a mule driver on a farm near Andújar all his life. He wears a patch on his chest that reads, *Stop, bullet, for the Sacred Heart of Jesus is with me,* and, beneath the collar of his army jacket, a scapular. A good soldier *and* a good Christian! Questioned by this reporter, as deadly bullets flew— a furious torrent of steel raining down on our martyrs' flesh—he, indifferent to the danger, and with exemplary modesty, made light of his heroic feat, recorded in the annals of history with letters of gold. "I was just doing my duty. I couldn't lose that mule; she'd been entrusted to me. And when I saw that group of Marxist soldiers, I did what anyone would have done: I ordered them to surrender. And now here they are, at the Glorious National Command's disposal."

I bid farewell to Corporal Castro with a manly handshake, feeling the calluses on his warm palm. Here stands Viriato's progeny; here stands the valiant fortitude of the ancient Celtiberian race. This is a Spaniard. This is a soldier. This is a man.

Castro finishes the article and folds the paper. *Jesus Christ.* He remains pensive. *Jesus Christ! You shit your pants at the sight of a combat jacket, Castro. So why the fuck did you ever talk to that guy? Now look at the mess you're in.*

A liaison from the second company passes by.

"What's up, Castro? You in a daze or what?"

"Huh? Oh, it's nothing, man," he replies distractedly.

Castro goes back to the command room, head bowed. "May I, Commander?" he inquires humbly from the doorway.

"Come on in, Corporal."

The officer looks pleased. Here comes a reprimand and, unless there's some kind of divine intervention, an arrest.

"Commander, sir, I didn't tell the reporter any of the stuff he wrote. I told him that the reds surrendered to me and that I didn't do a thing, 'cause they thought if they switched sides during the attack, they'd be better off as prisoners if they followed a nationalist."

The commander is smiling broadly. "Did you come on Captain Montero's horse?"

Castro falters. Now, on top of the whole newspaper ruckus, there's going to be an even bigger to-do because he used army property for his own ends.

"Yes, Commander. She's outside. I've almost got her broken in."

"Let's go take a look."

The commander admires the mare, pats her neck. "Good girl, good girl." He turns to the corporal. "You've done a good job, Castro. Who taught you to break in horses?"

"My father, Commander, sir."

"You're a clever kid, you learn fast. Now, pay attention: I know what happened with the reds, and I know you told the truth in your report. And that's to your credit, Castro. But you have to understand that the current situation is ... delicate. It means a lot for the nationalists and, as such, requires your compliance."

"But, Commander, what that man says in his—"

The commander raises his hand and looks into Castro's eyes. "That's an order," he warns sharply.

Corporal Castro stands at attention.

"Yes, sir, Commander, sir. It's not for me to decide. It's just that I don't like lying to people, sir."

Commander Soler nods, placing a fatherly hand on Castro's shoulder.

"I know, Castro. I know you're a good man. But people need heroes at a time like this. We've been at war three years, and everyone's tired of suffering and hardship. You'll be doing your nation a great service if you learn that story by heart and tell it just like it says when people ask you about it."

"Whatever you say, Commander."

"How long has it been since you went to Córdoba?"

"I went on my leave, Commander."

"Well, you're going again today to introduce yourself to Lieutenant Afín of the Military Government. Check out the travel connections, then talk to my assistant to arrange for your leave and the money you'll need."

"Yes, sir!"

The truck leaves in half an hour. Castro finds Chato in the quartermaster's depot.

"Chato, I'm going to Córdoba and I don't know when I'll be back."

"Now that's luck, you son of a bitch!"

"Luck, maybe, but whether it's good or bad . . . we'll just have to see where it leads. They put me in the paper after what happened the other day."

"Good thing you're getting out of here, 'cause things are about to get a lot worse. Did you hear the reds opened a six-mile breach from Cerro del Médico to Sierra Trapera? I heard a guy from the Twenty-first Soria say that some of the Trapera companies lost *all* their men."

"Jesus," says Castro. He looks at Chato, at a loss for words. "Will you watch the mules for me while I'm gone?"

"Course I will. I'll take special care of Valentina. Just have a good time. And bring back some tobacco and chorizo, will you?"

Castro pats his friend's arm and walks to the quarter-master's truck, then jumps in the back. Two soldiers raise the tailgate and bolt it shut.

"We're off!" the driver calls.

The mechanic cranks the motor to start the engine. He tilts his cap back and settles in beside the driver.

Castro—sitting on a bundle of empty sacks, grabbing on to a hanging chain so as not to lose his balance over potholes and curves, both of which the driver takes at high speed—reflects on everything that's happened in the past few weeks. He lost his girlfriend, almost lost

Valentina, his friend Second Lieutenant Estrella was wounded, and now, suddenly, he's been turned into a national hero, without so much as lifting a finger.

Halfway there, at a health spa in Fuenteagria that's now being used as an aid station, they stop to load empty baskets onto the truck. Convalescing patients stroll beneath huge eucalyptus trees, some in wheelchairs pushed by nurses in white pinafores and blue blouses.

Castro asks to see Second Lieutenant Estrella. He's directed to the second room on the left and enters, much to the surprise of his friend.

"Holy shit, Castro! What're you doing here?" Estrella exclaims.

"On my way to be decorated—I suppose you read about my incident in the newspaper."

"I sure did." Estrella pauses. Neither man is comfortable discussing the politics the event has stirred, the "moral victory" over the reds it implies. "And your girlfriend? How does she feel now with a famous man such as yourself?"

Castro looks at the floor. "When your words left my letters, sir, she left me."

"Castro, I'm sorry. But now you won't need me for help." Estrella turns to a nurse. "Marisa, this is my friend, the one in the paper."

"*Ay!* The man from the newspaper is here!" the nurse shouts to the entire unit.

A throng of nurses, health workers, and doctors cluster around to meet the hero. They overwhelm him with questions. Some take their pictures with him.

"What was it like?"

"Just like it said in the newspaper. I got real lucky."

A pretty nurse hugs him and kisses his cheeks.

"Oh, thank you, Corporal! You're a real source of pride to our troops! May God protect you!"

Then she plants two more kisses on his face and gives him a big hug; he can feel her hard, swollen breasts press up against him. Castro blushes; in fact, he's beginning to enjoy his new role.

Settling back into the truck, Castro eats two oranges that another nurse slipped into his pockets. He smiles. *If only my mother could see me,* he reflects for a moment. *No, actually it's better if she doesn't. I don't want anyone in Andújar to find out about this; it could cause more trouble for my father. Wait 'til the war's over.* He pictures his return to La Quintería, his chest full of medals, the hero who went out to rescue a mule from enemy territory and came back with ten prisoners and a submachine gun.

He's lost in this fantasy as the truck takes one final curve, and then Córdoba appears on the plain in the distance, with its bell towers and gardens, its palm trees and river groves.

Córdoba.

Chapter 21

In the halls of the Córdoba Military Government, currently housed in an old Carmelite convent, officers of every rank and branch of the armed forces charge to and fro, as do liaisons and orderlies ferrying papers and delivering cups of coffee. Castro, thrown by the activity, can't decide where Lieutenant Afín might be. He pauses to admire the fountain in the central courtyard, where a parsimonious trickle of water flows from an upturned bronze faucet.

"Top floor, all the way at the back," replies the soldier he finally dares to ask for the Office of Press and Propaganda.

He climbs the tiled stairway and walks past the half-open door of a room in which General Queipo de Llano himself is addressing a group of journalists.

"I'm going to give you the ideological foundations of the new State..." he begins.

The famous general has just arrived from Sevilla to lead the Peñarroya counteroffensive in person. While Queipo explains the establishment of the new State—born of the victory of the wholesome army over the rotten faction of the Spanish populace—Corporal Castro wanders down the convent halls, lost, envying the lucky bastards in the champagne unit who finagled postings here. Everywhere he looks, he sees well-polished boots, well-cut army jackets and trousers, rosy faces, and carefree warriors who've seen no war, who live in a world of papers and telephones, who sleep in soft beds, neither hungry, nor cold, nor scared. "Christ, Valentina, who do you have to know to get posted to a place like this?" Castro says to himself. The Marquis of Pineda, don Federico, would surely have found him a cushy job like this, far from the front, if he weren't waiting out the war in Bia...Bia... "Well, anyway, girl, let's play our luck and drag this out 'til the war ends."

Castro addresses a pen-pusher who's stopped to organize the papers in his notebook, one foot in the air like a stork. "Excuse me, I was told to report to Lieutenant Afín in the Office of Press and Propaganda."

The soldier glances at the official letter in Castro's hand.

"Over there," he says, looking back at his stack of papers. "Second door."

The Office of Press and Propaganda is located in a cramped room beneath the imperial staircase, barely large enough for two desks, their occupants, and a sawed-off bookshelf fashioned to fit beneath the slanted ceiling.

Lieutenant Afín, delicate-looking and immaculate, is wearing glasses, a blue shirt, and riding boots with spurs. He peruses the official letter declaring that the individual bearing it is Juan Castro Pérez, and then examines Castro with interest.

"So you're the one who captured ten militiamen."

"Yes, sir, Lieutenant. At your service."

The lieutenant looks at his watch and turns to the sergeant at the other desk.

"Pepe, call the garage. We're off. I'll be out the rest of the day. The Germans are in Las Ermitillas, right?"

"Yes, Lieutenant."

The lieutenant snatches his service cap from the hook and pulls it over his head at a jaunty angle, like a fashion model. An old black Ford awaits them at the door of the Military Government building.

"Corporal, you ride up with the driver."

Afín himself climbs into the backseat, on the right. He seems angry, but then, Castro has noticed that every weedy little officer adopts that look in an attempt to command respect. The driver glances at the lieutenant in the rearview mirror, awaiting orders.

"To Las Ermitillas, Paco. We're off to see the blond bombshell."

The driver beams and starts the engine. They drive through Córdoba. Peaceful, flint-paved streets, wet with rain, shine like patent leather. Lush green palms, willows, and mulberry trees peek over whitewashed walls. They drive through the gate leading to the Jewish Quarter and come out onto a wide avenue with banana palms and horse chestnuts. Almost no one is in uniform. Aside from a few patriotic signs and flags on military quarters, you'd never know there was a war on: Businesses are open; grocery stores are well stocked; cafés are packed with customers, particularly women. At the Alcázar wall, by the waterwheel, hangs a large poster of Generalísimo Franco wearing a helmet. Beneath him reads the caption, *Franco, El Caudillo, Savior of our Fatherland, Undefeated Leader of Eternal Spain. All Hail!*

Unbelievable, Castro thinks. *Now we pray to Franco like he was the Virgin Mary.*

He tries to remember the Hail Mary but gives up quickly. *In the war you lose everything, even your memory.*

Castro's thought a lot about Valentina on this trip. He trusts Chato, but he'd be powerless if they decided to do a count and discovered an extra mule. That'd be the end of it. And it would be *his* mule they'd take, the one he saved, the one he risked his life for. Chato would claim she was from another company, brought in to be treated. But Valentina's been healthy for months now, yet Castro hasn't returned her to her unit. Castro tries to banish the gloomy thoughts from his mind. *Everything will be fine,* he tells himself. *Besides, why worry when I've become a hero? They're even going to give me a medal! Better enjoy life while I can. Who knows what hell there might be to pay before the war ends. Look at poor Lieutenant Estrella, with a leg full of shrapnel.*

Lieutenant Afín interrupts these reflections to tell him what's expected of him.

A crew from UFA, the German Reich's film company, is documenting the war. They've fitted out some makeshift studios in a ruined *cortijo* a few miles from Córdoba, in Las Ermitillas. Teutonic technicians have managed to dress them up like a war-torn village. They dug a few trenches into a nearby hill, erected huts and barbed wire, and blew up a half dozen trees to simulate a military landscape. Castro's job is to reenact his victorious return to the nationalist lines with the mule and the Marxist prisoners.

The car pulls up by the old farmhouse's threshing floor, beside two other cars, a truck, and a van with a huge antenna. An icy north wind is blowing; taking shelter behind a parapet at the foot of a crumbled wall, fifteen or twenty men stand smoking, talking, and taking in what sun there is to be had. Some are dressed in militiamen's blue coveralls, leather or corduroy jackets, service caps with republican bars, and one or two Adrian helmets with a central crest. Others wear nationalist garb, with blanket capes and forage caps. A few wear *jellabas,* turbans, and fake beards, their bare legs shivering in the open air.

The director is a corpulent man, strawberry blond with a crew cut, his head shaved at the temples. A couple of poorly healed scars ruin an otherwise good face. A monocle, attached by a leather string to a buttonhole of his leather jacket, is wedged into his right eye. A young blonde secretary shadows him. She's a buoyant, towering young Valkyrie trying to hide her shapely figure—to the degree possible—by clutching the script in front of her generous bosoms. The director greets Lieutenant Afín with a click of his heels; Afín responds by energetically raising his hand to the peak of his cap, a military salute designed to show the blonde what kind of men Spaniards really are.

"This is our man, *Herr* Kriegskartoffeln." The lieutenant points to Castro. "Juan Castro Pérez, corporal muleteer."

The German looks at Castro as if he were an exotic animal. He walks around him.

Castro stands at attention and salutes. When in doubt, he always salutes. The man with the monocle might not be military, but he carries a martial air.

"So, this is the Spaniart hero." The German sighs and clucks his tongue, disappointed. "Not vat vee ver expectink. You say 'expectink,' yes?" he adds, examining the corporal. "He is little, runtlike, unt not very attractif—in fact, not at all. He does no justice to the noble Spaniart race. Unt besites, he's too dark. Have you no soldier vith better skin, lighter?"

"I'm sorry, *Herr* Kriegskartoffeln," Lieutenant Afín begins, "but this is the man himself, the hero who defeated an entire platoon of reds. Besides, you've probably noticed that a certain sector of the Spanish race is rather short and unimposing." He winks. "That's because their balls drag them down!"

Herr Kriegskartoffeln laughs uproariously, displaying large, intensely white teeth and one gold filling, the kind Mohammed yanks out of dead soldiers' mouths. He wipes a tear and shrugs.

"Okay, if vee must film vith him, vee'll film vith him!" he concedes.

He faces the crew and barks orders at two or three cameramen and the lighting technicians.

Sergeant Morales—a noncommissioned officer from the Office of Press and Propaganda, currently serving as a prop man—preps the set. Those dressed as reds—grim and unshaven, wearing leather jackets and Russian caps sporting inaccurately large red stars, carrying enormous pistols on their belts—saunter toward the camera, arms aloft, acting submissive. They're followed by Corporal Castro, who's brandishing a Russian submachine gun that they went through endless red tape to borrow from the regional military gunsmith's commander in chief.

When the set is readied and they've run through the

motions a couple of times, *Herr* Kriegskartoffeln shouts, "Let's roll! Brink out the mule!"

"The mule, the mule!" the sergeant acting as director's assistant shouts unnecessarily. *Probably justifying his posting,* Castro thinks.

One of the soldiers in Moorish costume—*jellaba* and slippers—leads a small, hairy, Cordovan donkey with enormous twitchy ears.

"A *donkey?*" Lieutenant Afín asks quizzically. "What Corporal Castro saved was a *mule,* wasn't it? The corporal's a *mule* driver."

"Yes, sir," Sergeant Morales apologizes, "but the three regimental mules were unavailable. All we could find was this donkey. One of my relatives has a farm near here and he lent him to me. We have to have him back by dark, 'cause he still has to cart a few loads of water."

The lieutenant glances at his watch again. He's arranged to meet a telephone operator in Café Calipso at seven o'clock: They're going to the movies. He wants to finish up here as quickly as possible so he can get home and wash his nether regions, in case he gets lucky.

"Oh well, mule, donkey, what's the difference? It's the thought that counts!" he suddenly concedes. "Castro, get the donkey and lead it in for the camera, behind the prisoners."

Castro obeys. What does he care? The prisoners trudge by the camera behind the barbed wire, looking beaten, their hands held high; then Castro follows with the donkey and the submachine gun.

"Cut, cut!" *Herr* Kriegskartoffeln shouts. "Terrible! This donkey—vat is this? Vee cannot show this to the German public, to the Reich spectators! There vill be ladies, children, young girls! Even the Führer himself, unt he's very circumspect—is that the right vort? This donkey, ach!"

"What's wrong with the donkey?" Sergeant Morales wonders.

"Can't you see?"

Herr Director points to the anomaly. The animal has let his equipment drop and is exhibiting a rather overstated testimony to his virility, which nearly reaches the ground.

The extras elbow one another, giggling, until the irate lieutenant wheels around to face them, furious, cutting them short. The cherubic Valkyrie looks on with disdainful indifference, as if the whole business has nothing to do with her. She's quite used to arousing the base instincts of boorish Latin types and accepts it as one of the many indignities she's forced to endure to serve her country and her beloved Führer.

"We'll just have to wait for him to put it away, Lieutenant," Sergeant Morales proclaims with professional objectivity.

They all stand there waiting, but after thirty seconds

the ass's display of force has not waned in the slightest. The lieutenant looks at his watch again.

"Well! The little donkey certainly can't complain about his health!"

Herr Kriegskartoffeln wheels to face Castro.

"You! You are a mule driver! An animal specialist! A donkey engineer! It is your duty to fix this! Do somethink!"

"What is it with this German? Does he think we're all idiots?" Castro points to the ass, which, not content with simply displaying his prowess, begins hamming it up, with a sort of pendular swaying equivalent to beating his chest. "May I, Lieutenant?"

"For goodness sake, man, yes. Do something!"

The Valkyrie has discreetly retired to the background and leans against the van, out of eyeshot, while following the donkey's gymnastics with interest.

Castro glances at his audience, lights a cigarette, and saunters over to the ass, without removing the cigarette from his lips. The animal keeps up his show of strength. Castro gets close enough to his ear for the tip of his cigarette to touch the sensitive skin of the inner ear, singeing it. The painful stimulus causes the donkey to sheathe his member with astonishing celerity.

"This is amazink!" *Herr* Kriegskartoffeln exclaims. "You must tell me, vat did you visper to the donkey?"

"You want me to tell him, Lieutenant?" Castro asks.

"Yes, yes! Tell him; we all want to know!" Afín urges.

"I told him to put his dick away quick, 'cause that guy with the glass in his eye wants to suck it."

"I don't understant!" *Herr* Kriegskartoffeln cries.

"Oh, it doesn't matter, *Herr,*" the lieutenant intercedes, chuckling. "He simply told him to act civilized in the name of the Hispano–German alliance."

Satisfied, *Herr* Kriegskartoffeln claps twice.

"Vee continue!"

"Everybody, places! We're going to reshoot the capture," the sergeant thunders. "You, donkey guy, try to stand in front of him so he doesn't see the honeypot over there and get another stiffy. Looks like this animal doesn't miss anythink!"

They film the prisoners behind the barbed wire a few more times before *Herr* Kriegskartoffeln approves.

Lieutenant Afín bids the German farewell.

"*Herr* Director, please forgive me. Serious business requires my presence back at headquarters."

"Please. Go, go! Var von't vait!"

They climb back into the Ford. The driver starts the engine and they begin the trip back. The lieutenant slaps his shoulder.

"She's gorgeous, that German, eh?"

The driver glances in the rearview mirror.

"Gorgeous? Pretty as a picture, Lieutenant. And I'd nail her to the wall!"

Chapter 22

January 11, 1939. Fourth Triumphal Year. If not for the pitch black, Castro could see a gentle rain falling over the fallow fields, olive groves, orchards, sleeping towns, grade crossings, rivers, and streams. From his window seat in the third car of the Córdoba mail train, life seems nicer somehow. In one pocket of his brand-new army jacket—issued at the Córdoba quartermaster's—he's stashed a ticket to Los Rosales station. In the other rests the pass authorizing him to travel to Burgos, to the administration offices of the Generalísimo's headquarters, and the five hundred *pesetas* he was given upon presentation of the required receipt, in triplicate, from the office of the paymaster general of Córdoba's Military Government.

Castro's happy: He's far from the front; all his clothes,

including his boots and underwear, are new; he's got more money in his pocket than he's ever had in his life; and he's seeing the world, an experience he had no idea he'd enjoy so much. This is the first advantage he's found to the war. People like him, who would ordinarily see the same old horizon every day, now get to travel Spain. All thanks to the war. *Shame we can't do this in peacetime,* he thinks.

Castro's going to Burgos to be decorated for his bravery by Franco. In person. The Generalísimo of the National Army, Caudillo of Spain. When he sees posters of Franco at the train stations, he can't help but look down at his chest, above his left pocket, to where the Caudillo's own hands will pin a medal of valor in just a few days. Thinking about it, Castro's slightly ashamed. *Valentina, I never really showed any valor. Unless going to find you during a battle is courageous. But I can't help it if that's how they want it to be. I'm just going to do like Chato says: keep my mouth shut, let the commanders command, and hold a gun in my hand. Chato . . . this is the first time we've been apart since the war started. I hope he does everything right and takes care of you, Valentina. It's about time for all three of us to get back to Andújar.*

He fingers his jacket pocket and wonders if he'll be robbed once he falls asleep. It wouldn't be easy. His money is in an envelope in his shirt pocket, which is buttoned and safety-pinned, for extra security. He's also got twenty-five *pesetas* and some loose change for sundries in his wallet, which is in his pants pocket.

The train is full of soldiers on leave, so raucously happy that no one can sleep through their wine-swigging and rowdy singing of the "*Carrasclás*" anyway.

Castro gets off the next morning in Los Rosales. His connection to Villanueva del Río y Minas is a truck fitted out like a bus, covered with a canvas top; two church pews are bolted down for the passengers' comfort. The space between them has a smoking coal brazier screwed onto a metal plate to keep the travelers from freezing.

It's stopped raining and the day is overcast and ugly. The truck stops briefly in Tocina, in the plaza, where the passengers who can afford it have *churros* and chicory for breakfast underneath a market stall. Those who can't take seats closer to the brazier.

At the Villanueva del Río y Minas station, Castro watches a slowly maneuvering mining train make room for the one pulling in. Just after nine o'clock, his La Viajera train bound for Extremadura via El Pedroso and Guadalcanal departs, thirty minutes late. Perched on his uncomfortable wood-slat seat, burrowed into his new army jacket, Castro watches the scenery go by: green hills, kermes oaks, ilex oaks, cork oaks, clearings full of wet grass, puddles, and ponds that hardly even shimmer in the pale, grimy light of the grim day. When they reach the Zafra station, Castro shows his pass, buys another ticket, and joins the throng of people crowded onto the platform. It's sometime after twelve when the Northern Express arrives, an hour late and packed, passengers crowding the aisles, doorways, and open-top cars. Only soldiers with passes are allowed on. After pushing his way through, Castro finds a spot in an open-top car. Two hours of intense cold later—shivering beneath his blanket cape, his lapels upturned, cap pulled down to his eyes— he manages to find a place inside, when they're almost to Cáceres. While they're stopped, waiting for the engine to be refilled with water and coal, hordes of women selling pork pies and anise assail the passengers.

"Delicious anise, one *real,* just one *real,* get your anise here! Warm you right up!" cries a pretty, self-assured girl.

It's clear she's suffered her share of blows without having ever been on the front.

"Can't I offer you a glass of anise, Sergeant?" she asks Castro.

"All right, then."

Castro takes the tiny cup and gives her a *peseta.*

"Keep the change, gorgeous."

He's feeling lavish, the five hundred *pesetas* burning a hole in his pocket.

"Want another, Colonel? My treat," she says, staring into his eyes.

Castro feels himself blush.

"If not, I'll take it," replies the gray-haired Roma sitting beside him, baring two gold teeth.

He'd told Castro earlier that he supplied the army with horses.

"Let this gentleman have it."

The girl pours a drink for the horse trader, who gulps it down and licks the glass, staring at her lasciviously.

The clerk's whistle blows. The train shudders to life, then pulls out. Castro leans out the window to look at the girl again, who's making her way through the crowd.

"Terrible thing, the war, don't you think?" an old man seated opposite him asks.

"You said it."

"I have two sons, just like you, enlisted. So far, they've made it through unharmed."

The old man crosses himself. He's wearing an aluminum Virgin of Carmen pendant on his collar. Instead of a shirt, he wears a purple habit.

The train trundles through a rocky landscape of dwarf oaks and flooded meadows where scrawny, exhausted-looking bulls graze. They pass a few shacks in the clearings; destitute families and half-naked children run out, shouting, "Give us something!" to the passengers in the open-top cars.

The old man has announced he's going to recite some of his poetry, to make the journey more pleasant for the distinguished passengers. And so he begins.

Though I'm just a peasant
And that's always what I'll be
In my old age I write poems
For our great nation's glory.
So listen to my verses

Pay attention to my song
For the lines that I recite you
From my heart they come along.
Here in this lovely train car
I can see so many oaks
Olive and carob trees too
Even butcher's broom, folks

"That's right!"
"You tell it, now!"
A middle-aged woman holding a wicker basket containing a rambunctious chicken applauds.

The old man smiles and holds up his hand in a request for silence.

We're all born into this world
And our mothers' love we take
And some men put on war boots
But the rest can jump in the lake

"Hold on a minute, there! That sounds commie to me!" one passenger remarks.

"What are you talking about?" the old man snaps. "I'm part of the movement, I'll have you know! You just didn't understand it properly. Here, let me recite another one where you can tell more clearly."

A man with his own riches
They're his, and that's his right.

No other man can shoot him
If he's poor and full of spite

"There. You see?"

"That's better," admits the doubtful passenger, now satisfied.

"Why don't you write a verse for the train?" the woman asks.

"The train? Let's see, now..."

It travels through the low hills
And passes a deep spring,
And crosses through the scrubland
Where the warm mountains sing

"Lovely! That's lovely!"
Several passengers clap.
"And now, let me recite one I wrote for the Caudillo."

To the Caudillo who saved us
From those godless, evil men
We love the glory he gave us
And the sentence he gives them.
Their backs against the wall
They're shot and then they fall

Chapter 23

After two days on the train, suffering interminable stops in Béjar, Salamanca, and Valladolid, Castro watches day break over his destination, Burgos: Pointy gray roofs and black towers emerge from the mist like knives stabbing the sky.

Castro's finally there. The Express stops beneath the station's wood and iron shelter. It's plastered with nationalist posters, almost entirely images of Franco in various inimitable poses, sometimes sporting a helmet, sometimes a service cap. Throngs of uniformed men from every unit of the national army crowd the platform and surrounding premises. Several girls in blue blouses and black wool tights are serving coffee and *magdalena* cakes to wounded soldiers who are resting in the confines of an improvised enclosure with folding chairs and luggage.

Castro bids farewell to his fellow passengers, slings his knapsack over his back, and steps off the train. He takes out the official letter in his pocket: *Report to the administration offices of the Burgos Military Government.*

Approaching a sergeant, Castro stands at attention and then asks for the administration offices. Before replying, the sergeant takes his time, reading the letter all the way through.

"That's easy, Corporal. Just exit the station, take that avenue all the way down, turn right at Calle General Sanjurjo, and then at the...three, four, five...the fifth street turn left. When you get to the plaza, you'll see it. A large building with flags and sentries at the door. Just report to the sergeant on duty."

"Yes, Sergeant!"

It's after twelve by the station clock, which is slow. Castro hurries. He most certainly doesn't want to miss a free lunch. He's going to save as much of the five hundred *pesetas* as he can, since the war's practically over—any day now. That money is going to come in very handy to help out his family. He's already decided to buy dresses for his mother and his sisters, Jacinta and Manuela. Castro doesn't know what's become of Manuela's husband, whether he's back home yet. She might need money for her three kids. Whatever the case, he'll find out soon enough.

The building has a flag, sentry box, and cannon at the door, with a plaque that reads: *Seized from the reds at the glorious battle of the Jarama, February 17, 1937, Second Triumphal Year.* Castro walks through an inner courtyard adorned with a fountain and potted aspidistras and finds the administration offices. A fat lieutenant, whom Castro would just love to actually see working the trenches, greets him. Castro stands at attention, waiting for the officer to read the letter.

"So you're the soldier from Córdoba? Well, good thing you're here. We were expecting you yesterday. The ceremony is tomorrow. Report to Captain Suanzos, upstairs, second door on the right."

Captain Suanzos is a frail-looking fifty-year-old, pasty from lack of sunlight, with a pencil-thin mustache. In an upholstered leather *frailero* chair, beneath a portrait of the Generalísimo and the national flag, he sits reading a newspaper, which is spread out on an enormous wooden table carved with all manner of military motifs: morion helmets, cannons, long antique rifles with fine bayonets, ramrods, scimitars, sabers, spears...a veritable scrapyard exquisitely carved into the fine wood desk used to support the officer's telephone.

Captain Suanzos examines the letter the soldier hands him, and, upon realizing he's face-to-face with the heroic Corporal Castro, he stands, skirts the table, and shakes his hand vigorously.

"An honor to meet you, Corporal! Your heroism will

forever be inscribed in the annals of our Glorious Army. Now, report to Lieutenant Pardillo and he'll show you to your lodgings."

Corporal Castro descends the imperial stairway. The lieutenant isn't in, but a young second lieutenant leads him to a dormitory with seven cots, each with a locker, and seven sinks lined up against the wall, each with a towel hanging on a peg. The entire back wall is covered by a gaudy mural depicting an idealized battle scene: tanks, planes, cruisers, and armies. A huge crucifix hangs over the mural, and, when viewed straight on, the bottom of the cross appears to be emerging from the crotch of one of the fallen soldiers. The whole scene is completed by an inscription in Gothic-style calligraphy—the first letter of each word in red and the rest in black—which declares: *The brave soldiers of the Glorious Spanish Army may die, but they will never surrender. Donoso Cortés.*

"This Donoso guy must be connected. Probably another one who's never set foot in the trenches." Castro is beginning to find himself annoyed by the sight of so many uniforms so far from the front.

"Just like a hotel, eh?" the second lieutenant remarks. "Settle in, then come on down to the dining room, where I'll introduce you to the others."

The "others" are six more heroes whom Franco will also be decorating: a Moor from the Moroccan regular platoon wearing a fez and slippers, who, having been shot twice himself, carried his wounded captain out of the fray; a second-lieutenant pilot who sank a red merchant ship that was about to unload supplies in the Barcelona port; a navy corporal who's machine-gunned three planes to date; a Falangist volunteer in blue shirt and belt, the only survivor of a unit that took an enemy parapet in the Ebro operations; a Carlist wearing a red beret—and a patch that reads, *Stop, bullet, for the Sacred Heart of Jesus is with me*—who, armed with only a spade, managed to decapitate a red commander in hand-to-hand combat; and, completing the tableau, a sergeant from the Legion, who rendered a Marxist tank useless.

"He climbed up, forced the hatch open with a tire jack, and tossed in a Lafitte hand grenade," the second lieutenant explains by way of introduction.

The man in question raises his hand dismissively. "Any Legion man would do the same."

Seven heroes, each representing one arm of the Glorious National Army, whom the Generalísimo himself will decorate during a solemn ceremony.

"Here's the missing man," the second lieutenant introduces Castro. "The corporal here wiped out an entire platoon of reds on the Córdoba front and brought ten prisoners back."

Castro obediently nods in corroboration with the newspaper article.

"Well done, Corporal!"

"Now that's what I call *cojones*!" the second lieutenant cries. "What do you do in peacetime?"

"I'm a muleteer, Lieutenant, and I'm also pretty good at pounding esparto."

"Civilian skills are good," the second lieutenant states, "but I bet you're thinking about reenlisting in the army. Daredevils like you are born to restore Imperial Spain to its glory!"

"Uh, sure."

A kitchen corporal informs them it's chow time, and the seven heroes take their seats at the dining table. Two white-jacketed waiters set down a large pot, and the cook serves them each a generous helping of lamb stew.

"Hope you like it, 'cause this is a one-course meal. You can have as much as you want, of course. And there're bananas for dessert."

He looks at the Moor. "And don't you worry, this lamb stew is made from good Spanish sheep, no *jalufo,* eh?" He looks at the officer and explains, "That's Arab for pork, Lieutenant. Arabs are ignorant by nature, so they won't eat it; that's just the way they are. Don't drink wine either, poor fools."

They relax for an hour after lunch before being loaded into a truck and driven to the regional quartermaster's depot. There, each man is issued a new uniform corresponding to his corps. An army tailor—who's also sergeant major—hems the navy corporal's trousers: None of the standard sizes fit the sailor's puny physique.

"Sergeant Major, what do you think about these jacket

tails?" he asks, glancing in the mirror. "They're a little long, see? It looks more like an overcoat."

"Pretend it's a three-quarter length," the tailor snaps with military severity. "I can't restitch all that now, the day before you meet the Generalísimo! I can't make miracles out of thin air!"

The corporal resigns himself, and the second lieutenant comes back in.

"Everybody ready? Superb. Now back to the barracks; I want everyone in bed early—there's a lot going on tomorrow."

They're taken back to the barracks, where the sergeant stays with them in order to ensure they don't get drunk.

Tucked up in bed, Castro imagines yet again his return to La Quintería: his uniform, Franco's medal pinned on his chest, people greeting him on the street, hugging him, with Valentina trailing along behind. He holds back his tears and feels the sweet breathlessness that accompanies intense emotion, a tender lump in the throat.

The next day there's no need to sound the reveille. Everyone is already up and out of bed, ready to shower before breakfast. The lieutenant orders them to fall in and passes inspection in the courtyard.

"Let me see those hands! Fingernails! Good. Clean, that's how I want 'em! Fall out and get on the bus."

They go outside and the lieutenant glances at the sky, slightly less overcast than the day before. He rubs his hands together.

"Those clouds are nothing; it's clearing up!" he exclaims. "God is on our side. This is just what we need for a formal religious military ceremony."

On the way, the bus picks up three tall, blond, handsome German aviators from the Condor Legion and two reedy, smiling, extroverted Italians from the Corpo Truppe Volontarie, who wear helmets with pheasant feathers. They drive along the tree-lined bank of the Arlanzón River, leaving the gardens of Cartuja behind. After a few miles of flat open road, they come to a long stone wall. On the other side they stop at a raised platform, beside which half a dozen glimmering automobiles are parked, some with generals' ensigns and chauffeurs standing beside them. A general staff captain comes out to greet them, and the lieutenant has them fall in and stand at attention. The captain greets the lieutenant.

"Is this the troop?"

"Yes, Captain."

"All here?"

"All here, Captain. Here's the list."

"Excellent! Follow me."

They trot along after the captain, who takes them to an area set off from the stage.

"Listen up: I'm going to run through the ceremony with you. The building you see behind me here is Las

Huelgas monastery. First, there will be an open-air Mass, on that courtyard over there, led by the general army chaplain. If any of you want to confess, you'll have five minutes. Where's the Moor"—he glances down at his paper—"Corporal Mohammed Siufiya?"

"Yes, sir!" the man in question says, saluting.

"Good. Since you're Muslim, you're exempt from Mass and Confession. You take a walk around the parking lot and pay attention; I want you right back here the minute it ends. And don't dirty your uniform or I'll take the rod to you, is that clear? The rest of you . . ." He glances at the Germans. "You Catholic?"

The three nod, having no idea what he's said.

"Good. In that case, everyone else to Mass. When it's over, the army chaplain will step down. Then comes the patriotic ceremony, which will consist of . . ." He extracts an index card from the top pocket of his army jacket to consult. "First, the army general's address; then a rousing speech by the Caudillo; third, the conferring of medals by the Caudillo—that's where you come in; fourth, closing remarks from the general secretary; fifth, the singing of the national anthem and cries for a free, united Spain, and, finally, fall out. Then they'll serve Spanish wine. When the ceremony and soiree are over, the same bus you came on will take you back to the barracks. You'll be free until tomorrow night, when you'll be given a pass to get back to your units. Now, fall out and pay attention to the lieutenant."

Chapter 24

The sky is overcast, and the monastery walls do almost nothing to mitigate the biting north wind. Led out by a lieutenant, the nationalist heroes march to the courtyard in perfect formation. The official ceremony will not begin for two hours and the dignitaries haven't arrived yet, but the company of honorees has been waiting—at ease—for some time already. Soldiers in work suits are finishing swathing the dignitaries' dais with maroon cloth, hanging flags, and rolling out carpets. In the very center lies a thick rug upon which sits a golden armchair with curved claw-foot legs, its seat back and cushion upholstered in maroon velvet.

Nearly one hundred high-ranking officers—from lieutenant colonel up—begin to arrive in cars and buses.

They wear pristine uniforms, shiny boots, and glimmering spurs. Their chests are studded with medals and decorations; some wear armbands, others have sashes, tassels hanging from them. Nearly all the civilians are dressed in coat and tails. Priests and prelates arrive as well, some in all black, others in red-trimmed black robes; there's even a cardinal in a red marbled-silk robe and bright cape.

Castro elbows the guy next to him.

"Check out the bishop. He left the lining of his cap on his head!"

The new arrivals search out friends and acquaintances, greet one another, stand at attention, salute with characteristic military rigidity, shake hands. Some give each other manly, back-slapping hugs. Then the men and particularly the ladies kiss the bishop's—and especially the cardinal's—rings. Generals' wives are dressed in evening gowns, and there's an entire retinue accompanying *Señora* Doña Carmen Polo de Franco. Castro sees young ladies in Falange uniforms, Welfare Service uniforms, Red Cross uniforms, even a few in deep-mourning black with *mantillas* or elegant hats.

"Get a load of that blonde over there," the antiaircraft naval officer says, pointing.

Castro immediately recognizes the film crew's Valkyrie from Córdoba.

"Damn, how'd the Germans *do* that? They were all in Córdoba five days ago! How'd they get here?"

"How do you *think*? They took the train?" the aviator

responds, laughing. "They flew in, genius. The planes are *theirs,* after all."

"Besides, it would've been dangerous to put a girl like that on the train," the legionnaire interrupts. "Men would have swarmed her. Christ, she's hot!"

A bugle sounds. The ceremony is about to begin. A sergeant major who's been posted at the entry to the platform flaps his arm to advise the colonel to send the honorees. The colonel passes the order down to the commander, who passes it on to the sergeant.

"Fall in, company!" the sergeant shouts.

The soldiers stop talking and stand at ease.

"Atten-*tion!*"

Three hundred well-trained heels click in unison; the sound echoes throughout the monastery grounds.

"I said *attention!*" the sergeant growls, his voice gruff. "Chests out, shoulders back. I want you stiff as dicks!"

He realizes, too late, that there are ladies present and shoots an apologetic glance over at the colonel, who returns an indignant expression with just the hint of a forgiving half smile.

The Caudillo is about to make his entrance. An air of expectation reigns, and everyone is stock-still except the bustling film crew. They've situated their cameras on a high stand, to the right of the official dais. One of Franco's liaisons approaches *Herr* Kriegskartoffeln and requests that his secretary move to a less visible place in the ladies' stand. *Herr* Kriegskartoffeln understands. If he leaves her there, in full view by the press box, she'll steal Franco's thunder: Those lascivious Spaniards will be unable to focus on the patriotic performance, the Mass, the rousing speeches, and especially the Caudillo.

The Caudillo's car, a huge black Mercedes with general's standards marking the front flag, makes its entrance from one side of the field. A captain, braids on his chest, signals the band leader, who returns to his troop and raises his conductor's baton. When he lowers it, the solemn strains of the national anthem begin. All conversation ceases immediately and the guests turn toward the president's box, standing at attention. The Mercedes pulls to a stop. The captain with braids on his chest opens the car door, salutes, and stands firm, hand frozen at his cap. The Generalísimo himself, shorter and darker than Castro had imagined him, steps out of the car, gazes over at the crowd assembled, and crosses the wide space quickly—with strides as long as his stumpy legs will allow—followed a few steps behind by a second lieutenant colonel, three generals, and half a dozen other lesser commanders. Each takes his place on the platform, Franco in the center, in front of the enormous maroon and gold armchair that makes him look even shorter than he already is. The crowd bursts into applause. Franco holds up a hand to call for silence, but a few tuxedo-clad guests at the back clap on for several more seconds: the bankers and industrialists who've prospered so much from the war. Franco then looks to the right and gives the quick nod that the second lieutenant colonel has been waiting for. He, in turn, gives the prearranged signal to the band leader. The band strikes up the "*Cara al Sol*," and everyone—military and civilian alike—stands at attention and listens, enraptured. When the hymn is over, Franco himself approaches the microphone and leads the chants—his voice clear, though shrill. The guests respond in unison.

"*¡España!*"

"*One!*"

"*¡España!*"

"*Great!*"

"*¡España!*"

"*Free!*"

"*¡Arriba España!*"

"*¡Arriba!*"

The Caudillo gives the microphone to the second lieutenant colonel, who steps forward and shouts—slightly hunched over, since the Caudillo hasn't stepped back enough to give him any room—"*¡Viva* Franco!*"

The responding cries of "*¡Viva!*" are even louder and more fervent than before, and are followed by thunderous applause that the Movement's newspapers will characterize as *a stentorian ovation*. Beneath his service cap, the Caudillo half-closes his eyes, obviously pleased, and returns to his place by the throne with quick, measured little steps—one, two, three—without turning his back to the crowd.

Overcome, Castro glances at the legionnaire. A ruthless,

hardened soldier—a "bridegroom of death," as they're
called—he is crying openly, the trails of two fat tears running down his tan, bony cheeks. Castro, too, is moved,
and feels the tiny hairs on his back and arms stand on end.

"Spaniards, you are about to have the honor of hearing
the sublime words of Francisco Franco, Caudillo of Spain
and Generalísimo of the Glorious National Army, Leader
of the Glorious National Movement!"

People applaud enthusiastically. Castro does likewise.

Directed by *Herr* Kriegskartoffeln, the film crew wheels
the huge contraption supporting the camera to film
the patriotic fervor with which the upper echelons of the
Movement welcome the Caudillo.

The colonel returns to his place; Franco steps to the
microphone again and raises a diminutive hand to call for
silence. A technician clad in an immaculate blue uniform
lowers the microphone to the Caudillo's height.

"Spaniards! Soldiers! Crusaders of Spain!" the Generalísimo's brash, high-pitched voice harangues. "In this
incomparable atmosphere, where the spirit is ennobled by
the purest essence of the Spanish military soul, in this
place sanctified by the military tradition of our Glorious
Fatherland, in this place where ancient kings and queens
who defended and expanded Spanish territory are buried,
we are going to decorate the heroes who have maintained
the dignity of our fatherland. In this Year of Victory, the
patriotic will of the wholesome faction of Spain has made
clear that—faced with the Marxist revolution called for by

naive fools who have fallen into the hands of the Godless, the Masonic, the Judeo–Marxist swine in the pay of Moscow—*our* will, that of the National-Syndicalists, shall rise to the top. *We* who unite the nation, who overcome historic hatreds, who eradicate barriers between the producer and the worker, the peasant and the mechanic, the soldier and the priest—the two highest offices in the fatherland. The dissolute republic, with its impracticable parliamentarianism, brought moral ruin to the fatherland. That time is over. The sturdy broom of New Spain will sweep it away. The days of crippled institutions are over.

"Now our ranks are firm and the spirited heart of Spaniards of order and righteousness lies in the institution. The National Movement has never been a rebellion. *They* are the rebels, they who corrupted the purest essence of the Spanish soul, who exchanged the gold coin of their patriotism for the Soviets' spare change. *They* are the ones who betrayed Spain. Our brave soldiers rose up to save her from the muck where she lay, to restore her to the throne of her imperial grandeur. Patriotism and Catholicism will be, from this day on, a way of life, a practice. Because our war is a religious war. We are not fighting man, we are fighting atheism and materialism; we are fighting all that degrades human dignity. In Spain there was once a militant Church, filled with warrior monks who fought to defend the faith. Now their time has returned. God has heard Spain. God shines His light on Spain. God and rea-

son are on the side of Spain, against all else, because Spain
has God's blessing...."

Two or three isolated bursts of applause don't manage
to spark the crowd off.

"... The red hydra had spread its tentacles throughout
Spain, but we have our nation's paladins right here: the
heroic soldiers who defeated that hydra. Today we will decorate a handful of brave soldiers. They have left comrades
in the trenches, and their comrades are in heaven. In the
January cold, many of them injured, their arms in slings,
their faces weather-beaten, these soldiers of Spain—the
best in the world—fought on, determined and stoic.
Victory is yours!"

Castro, despite his best attempt to make sense of the
profound doctrine Franco is emitting at this historic
moment—perhaps the most historic of his life—can't
keep his attention focused and finds his mind wandering
back to fantasies of his return to La Quintería. When he's
shaken from his reverie by applause, he hears Franco say:

"... but we are not alone in our endeavor, nor in our vi-
brant moment of victory. We are accompanied by comrades from sister lands. We offer heartfelt, warm regards
for our comrades in Italy, Germany, and Portugal, who
fight for civilization and against Asian barbarism, side by
side with our brave soldiers. This is the Year of Victory,
but that victory—which is now within our reach—is also
a promise of future peace, reconstruction, and harmony.

A future in which your Caudillo will not cease until there is no home in Spain without a hearth, no Spaniard without bread. I have spoken."

The Caudillo takes three ceremonious steps back; meanwhile, an ecstatic ovation nearly brings the place down.

Cries of "Franco! Franco! Franco!" ring out, chanted in unison by officers and troops alike. Castro thinks of Concha. He wonders where she is right now and if she knows that the Caudillo himself is going to decorate him. People must have shown her the newspaper article, she must have heard it on the radio. He pictures her snuggled up in bed, her hands between her thighs, perhaps regretting the blunder she committed by calling off a relationship with a true hero of the fatherland. Though he knows he didn't actually do anything heroic, he's gotten used to his role. *How many of the people we admire never really did what they're credited with?* he wonders. The memory of the last time he saw Concha warms his heart, despite her fury.

Just then, the bugle sounds for them to stand at ease. The ceremony is about to begin.

The colonel steps forward with a leather case embossed with the national eagle, which he opens and then announces, "And now, the Caudillo will decorate the heroes who have distinguished themselves on the battlefield."

Chapter 25

A maître d' appears, followed by three dozen waiters balancing drinks on silver trays. Despite their white jackets, it's obvious that the lackeys serving are soldiers: Their heads are shaved and they're wearing shiny boots. They scatter like guerrillas, slipping in and out among the guests, offering wine and fruit juice. One of them approaches the heroes, who are huddled in one corner like livestock in an unfamiliar pen.

"Here, take some before those guys drink it all."

Castro waits for the others to go first. He can't decide between wine and fruit juice. In the end, he takes the wine.

"This is nothing like the rat poison they give us in the trenches, eh?" the legionnaire comments.

Castro takes a sip and nearly chokes. He recognizes one of the nurses flirting with two boorish lieutenants: Pilarín, *Señorita* Cayetana's friend from Madrid whom Castro used to admire. When he's sure it's her, he gathers up his courage and approaches.

"*Señorita* Pilarín! Aren't you *Señorita* Pilarín?"

She turns toward Castro and glares, though her irate look is slightly tempered with curiosity.

"Yes, I'm Pilar Valbuena. Have we met?"

"Of course, *señorita*! Los Escoriales, in Las Viñas de Andújar? I'm Juanito, the one who took you to see the quails' nests."

It finally sinks in.

"Oh, sure! The Marquis of Pineda's stable boy! How are you? What a surprise!" She points to his decoration. "Wow, congratulations on your medal. You're a national hero!"

Castro blushes and stares at the floor.

"Oh, well, it's just . . . I was lucky," he stammers.

Pilar calls out to her friends, two other nurses and the two lieutenants.

"Hey, look at this! It turns out I know the corporal. . . . What was your name?"

"Juan Castro Pérez, at your service."

"Turns out I know him from a visit to Cayetana

Cañabate, the Marquis of Pineda's daughter, on her ranch in the Sierra Morena. What a surprise!"

They stare at the soldier, the nurses with vague curiosity, the lieutenants with envy that slightly dilutes the natural scorn felt by those who know that, no matter what, they come from superior stock. The medal the Caudillo conferred on him would look better on their immaculate, tailor-made uniforms than it does on this bumpkin's poorly cut, ill-fitting army jacket. But that's war for you. This bumpkin smacked into a gang of Marxists, took them down, and is being celebrated; they, serving hundreds of kilometers from the front, are unlikely to have such an opportunity.

"Is it true that Pilar shot an eight-point deer on the marquis's reserve?" asks one, pointing his glass of Rioja at the woman in question.

"Yes, Lieutenant, a very fine-looking deer it was too. A difficult shot, from a distance. But she shot it right through the heart. No need to finish him off."

"Well! *Caramba,* Pilarín!" the lieutenant exclaims, turning his back to Castro.

The nurses and lieutenants form a closed circle once more, excluding him. After a moment's hesitation, Castro returns to the group of decorated soldiers. They've finished their drinks and are waiting for another waiter to pass.

Instead, a sergeant arrives to distribute fine lacquered wood cases lined with velvet, in which to place their medals. Castro decides to keep his on his chest for now. The sergeant also gives them each two packs of American Lucky Strikes.

"You can head back to the barracks now," he says, pointing to the parking lot. "The bus is waiting. You've got the rest of the day off."

At the back of the grandstand, the band is launching into the military beats of the "Volunteers" march.

The decorated soldiers go onto the field-cum-parking lot, where groups of drivers stand chatting, oblivious to the party. On the other side of the gate, a crowd of enthusiastic patriots cheer for the Caudillo and give the fascist salute as they inhale the black smoke of the generals' cars.

"Corporal!"

Castro turns around. It's Pilar.

"Where are you rushing off to, Corporal?"

"I don't know, Pilar. To take a walk around Burgos, I guess."

She smiles. "I see you caught on. I don't like being called Pilarín."

"Yes, *señorita*. I could tell by the look you gave me."

"Cayetana used to call me Pilarín, but to these creeps I'm just Pilar. Would you like me to give you a tour?"

"Me?"

"Who else?" Pilar laughs at his ingenuousness.

"Of course I would, *señorita*!" Castro replies, both thrilled and flustered.

She looks into his eyes and smiles. "Can one man actually be so charming? And please, don't call me *señorita;* just Pilar."

Castro nods, his face flushed red.

She takes his arm familiarly. "Let's go!"

She turns to look back at one of the lieutenants from the group. Taller than the drivers, he stands with his legs slightly apart, cigarette in one hand, by the line of cars escorting the Caudillo, watching the scene unfold with carefree bemusement.

Castro feels she's trying to make the man jealous. Though he suspects he's being used and that her intimacy is insincere, the contact of a female arm still gives him a pleasant, lingering chill. He feels awkward but happy.

Pilar has a Fiat Balilla parked at the far end of the lot, a luxury car with leather seats and a lacquered-wood dashboard. She tells Castro to get in. Slipping the car into gear, she takes the main road, accelerates, and begins passing the lumbering mastodons in which the generals ride.

"Have you seen the cathedral?"

"No, *señorita.*"

"I thought you were going to call me Pilar," she scolds.

"Oh, that's right. Sorry, Pilar."

Pilar, what a beautiful name! Castro compares it to Abundia, to Concha, to his sisters Jacinta and Manuela. People from noble families seem to have the most extravagant names: Pilar.

She parks the Balilla in the cathedral square, beneath a huge poster of the Generalísimo in his steel helmet.

"Now, look at that," she says. "What do you think of the facade?"

Castro looks at the towers' latticework spires cutting through the gray sky.

"I can't believe they can make something like that out of stone. All those little details. Wonder how many paychecks that cost! And how'd they ever get the stones up that high?"

She gazes at him with a sort of disdainful interest. He might be a tiger in the trenches, but as soon as he's out of his element... What a lout. She's tempted to give him twenty-five *pesetas* and send him packing. But then she looks at his medal, glances discreetly down at his strong brown hands, and gives an involuntary shudder of carnal desire, contemplating the idea. Offering herself to a brute like him. Feeling how a worker does it, like an animal. The blood pounds in her temples.

"This is one of the greatest marvels of the world," she says, continuing with her explanation. "And let me tell you, I've seen a lot: I've been to Rome, France, Belgium, and soon I'm going to Germany! But there's no cathedral as pretty or colorful as this one."

They cross the square and enter the cathedral. It's dark inside. It smells of damp, of burned wax, of incense, of dead bodies. They walk in silence. Castro gawks at everything, spellbound, trying to affect respectful devotion. Women dressed in black, wearing shawls and coats, say the rosary in poorly lit chapels with votive candles. They continue on in a silence that Pilar breaks from time to time to whisper, "Look at that beautiful altar," "Look at that exquisite painting."

And eventually: "That's El Cid's tomb."

Castro looks at the little wooden coffer supported by two antique-looking iron miter joints.

"In such a small trunk?" Castro's dubious. "He must have just been a kid."

"Well, it *is* only his bones, you know."

"Oh!"

"He was as brave as you, but he waged war against the Moors."

"In Morocco?"

Pilar laughs heartily.

"No, not in Morocco, Juan. Here! When there were Moors *here*. Have you really never heard of El Cid?"

"Afraid not, *señorita*. We don't have a radio at home."

"Juan, it was never on the radio! El Cid is an old story, from back when there were Moors in Spain, over eight hundred years ago! He was the Catholic monarch's captain; he rid Spain of the Moors."

Pilar, amused, realizes just how naive—and how uncultured—the soldier is. A man who back in Los Escoriales had seemed so knowledgeable about nature, plants, rocks, ways to read the sky, a man who could tell edible hawthorn berries from the gooseberries that cause constipation, edible from poisonous mushrooms, a man who knew all about horses, who knew different types of deer by their names, who knew where birds' nests were and how many chicks each one had. . . . But as soon as you took him out of his environment he was lost in the world. Once or twice, almost by chance, she takes him by the arm and feels his rock-hard muscles. What must he be like in bed?

In the constable's chapel, as Castro is admiring the high, colossal ribbed dome ceiling and trying to work out how they covered it, Pilar watches the back of his dark neck, his young, weather-beaten skin, sunburned and hairy. She inches closer to his back and takes in his masculine scent, slightly acrid, like a horse or a wild animal: the smell of nature. Pilar is more accustomed to the aftershave and subtle colognes of the men she visits, all from illustrious families, hiding out at headquarters or occupying important posts in the rear guard.

She cuts the visit short. She'd been planning to wait for the *papamoscas* clock tower to strike, just to see Juan's reaction, but in her rush she decides to abandon this stage. On the way out she pretends to bump into him in the doorway and presses her large breasts against him. Castro blushes.

It's cold outside and the sky is clouding over.

"The weather's taking a turn for the worse," Pilar says. "We'd better get out of the open."

They go back to the car. Pilar takes Calle Paloma and parks in Plaza España.

"This is where I live."

"Well, thanks for the tour," he says, assuming this is where they'll part company.

"Come on up and I'll make you some coffee and a sandwich," she says. "I share an apartment with two other girls, two sisters, but they're in Salamanca today."

To Castro, this seems like a tremendous obstacle. She's alone, but she's asked him to come up. Perhaps a girl like her, modern and free, doesn't worry about social conventions. He looks down the street. Old people are sitting on benches in the plaza, leaning on their umbrella handles; convalescing soldiers are out strolling, accompanied by nurses. No one seems to be paying them any attention. Pilar opens the door and enters. Castro follows.

The magnificent entryway is lined with red and gray checkerboard marble tiles beneath a stuccoed ceiling. An elevator with a wrought-iron grille and a shiny brass panel of buttons waits at the end. Pilar lives on the second floor and never uses the elevator, but she guesses the corporal has never been in one. She slides the doors open decidedly and gestures, saying, "Get in."

Castro enters the narrow car hesitantly, testing the ground with his toe.

"It's not going to sink."

And Pilar smiles.

Is it disdain or sympathy in that smile? Either way, it's

class superiority. Castro, too dazzled by this overwhelming accumulation of sensations, lets himself be led along with self-conscious docility. He's aware of coming off as simple, discovering all of these new, extraordinary things that are part of everyday existence for privileged people like Pilar. A new world is unfolding before his very eyes. That remote, distant world glimpsed only in movies, in the darkness of the Trianón Theater in Andújar; but it's a real world, one that's right here, one that the war has placed within his reach. A world of airplanes, seven-story buildings with marble entryways and elevators; a world of automobiles, shiny shoes, gorgeous women, and dapper men; a world of beauty, luxury, and distinction; the same world he sensed that day the zeppelin floated over his herd of goats. The world of the Marquises of Pineda and their children, Virtudes, Federico, Cayetana, and Victoria, with their tennis rackets and their hunting rifles, their suitcases plastered with stamps from the best hotels in the world, with their swimming pool and their lawn. It was only natural: Of course they'd wage a war—die if necessary—to defend all that.

The elevator ascends slowly. Through the grille, the top of the cabin clicks past a tiny crosspiece on each floor, making it spin and whir. On the seventh floor, the elevator stops suddenly with a mechanical shudder. Pilar smiles and pushes the button for the second floor. The motor seems to exhale before starting again. This time the chain and counterweight rise and the car descends. When they reach the second floor, Pilar slides the doors open and they emerge. She takes a tiny key from her bag—another sign of progress—and opens the door. Inside the door is an entryway with a blue corduroy coat hanging on a hook, a large round mirror, an umbrella holder.

"Leave your jacket here," Pilar instructs.

Castro removes it on the spot.

The woman eyes him up and down, appraising. He's not very tall or very handsome, but he's well built. She doesn't know which excites her more, the idea of sleeping with a man who's killed reds or the social transgression of taking a worker to bed—an experience that, as far as she's aware, none of her friends has had. She wonders how the working class fucks. Are they as brutal as their lusty comments and animal-in-heat looks promise? She's seen them on the street, seen how they act toward refined women such as herself. Castro's a battle-worn soldier, his rough, stubby-fingered hands have taken men's lives. Pilar feels a sweet breathlessness in her throat. In a fit of passion, she takes the muleteer's head in her cold hands, feels his hot face, and places a soft kiss on his lips. Castro represses the desire to embrace her and feels a strong involuntary throbbing, the beginnings of an erection. He contains himself. How is he supposed to react in this situation? He can't treat her like one of Misangre's whores. She might get mad and send him packing. High-class women are moody. Better let her take the initiative.

Pilar takes his hand. They walk down a wide hall with

oil paintings of mustachioed men and hunting scenes on the walls. At the end of the corridor there's a suit of armor in one corner, like those in the comic books Federico used to leave forgotten beneath a dwarf oak back at Los Escoriales. Pilar pushes a door open and says, "This is the bathroom."

They're alone, but Pilar is whispering, and her voice has a hoarse catch to it.

It's spacious, with white tiles and a blue stripe around the border about five feet up the wall. In the center stands a huge iron claw-foot bathtub. A sink and large mirror, toilet and bidet line one wall. Castro thinks of Churri telling him, "I've eaten in palaces, with real silverware and bidets, requisitioned by the people."

"Now you're going to have a nice, invigorating bath," Pilar whispers. "Take off your clothes."

She turns on the tap, holds her hand beneath the flow, and when the water starts coming out hot, she puts the plug in. Castro watches. She's used to this. She probably takes a bath every day. A clean-smelling woman. That's the way rich people live; it's only natural.

"Start getting undressed and I'll get some towels," she says.

She leaves him there. Castro takes off his shirt and contemplates his hairy, muscular chest in the mirror, which is starting to steam up. His face and neck are brown, the rest of his body a milky white. He puffs out his chest, makes biceps. Is Pilar attracted to him? He takes off his pants, socks, underwear. Luckily it's all fresh and clean. He sniffs his sweaty armpits. Taking the bidet towel, he wets one corner and rubs his armpits, his back to the door. He's afraid she'll reappear any minute and catch him in the act, looking decidedly unmanly. He glances down; his erection is gone. Pilar comes back in wearing a robe and slippers, carrying an armful of towels. She looks at him standing there naked, his hands over his genitals, and smiles.

"You're not embarrassed in front of me, are you?"

"Um, well, a little."

"Well, then, I'm going to take my clothes off, too, so we're even."

She takes off her robe; she's wearing only panties now. Castro looks at her big, perky breasts, erect nipples, large pink areolas. The bathroom is completely steamed up. The white mist blurs their shapes. Pilar takes her panties off and hangs them on a hook. Castro inhales the steam, letting himself be led languidly along by these new sensations. She bends over to turn off the tap, presenting him with a great view of her magnificent ass. Is she expecting him to do something? Just in case, Castro represses his instincts. All he does is say, "You're the biggest lulu I've ever seen in my life."

She turns to him with an amused smile.

"Lulu?"

"I mean . . . you're a knockout."

"Ah, now I understand." Pilar laughs with that open smile. "Thank you. Now, get in the bath."

Castro climbs into the tub. The water is very hot but it feels good.

She kneels over the mat and scrubs him so hard with a soapy sponge it hurts. She takes her time with his penis and luckily rubs more gently there. Noting the beginning of an erection, she strokes him until he's completely hard.

"What does my little boy have here?" she asks, encircling his penis carefully and weighing it up with her long-fingered hand. "¡Caramba! Not bad. Not bad at all!"

She's seen a lot of naked men in her life, Castro thinks. *High-class women like her, they're free. Not uptight. And the guys who marry them don't care what they do. I wonder if that's better or worse than how us poor people think. If she was poor, Pilar would be considered a one-night tramp, but to rich people she's just a modern woman; she doesn't have to answer to anyone.*

He loses his erection suddenly when Pilar makes him bend over and slides a soapy hand between his buttocks, using one finger and taking her time with his anus. At first Castro's alarmed, but he relaxes when he realizes her intentions are more hygienic than sexual.

Pilar stands up. "Now I want you to dry yourself off with these towels."

She goes into the servants' bathroom, takes a toothbrush from the glass on the sink, and returns to the main bathroom.

"Here's a toothbrush for you; I want you to brush your teeth and tongue really well. Scrub hard. I'll put toothpaste on it for you, and you just see how fresh it makes your breath!"

For the first time in his life Castro brushes his teeth. He uses so much force under the woman's watchful eye that his mouth bleeds. Then he rinses his mouth with plenty of water from the stream gushing out of the sink.

The bedroom is across the hall. Pilar pushes him gently and whispers, "Get in bed and wait for me. I'll be right in."

It's a huge room, kept warm by two electric heaters. A sturdy canopy bed is presided over by a bas-relief of the *Sagrada Familia*. On the nightstand, a silver-framed photo of a young lieutenant, his cap set at a jaunty angle, a cynical white smile beneath a thin, carefully clipped mustache. *Boyfriend or brother? Won't she feel ashamed if she sees him watching her? Maybe she'll have a fit of remorse and everything will be ruined. Better if she can't see him.* Castro considers turning the photo to the wall or putting it facedown, but he stops himself. He doesn't know if that might anger her. High-class women get bent out of shape over anything. He's afraid to do anything that might spoil the night, which has started so promisingly. He gets into bed, pulls the covers halfway up his chest, and waits, listening to her ablutions in the bidet.

She appears naked: slightly droopy but bountiful breasts, pronounced waist, abundant velvety pubic hair. She closes the door, locks it, and runs to take refuge in the bed. They embrace. Castro kisses her shoulders and neck, noting that she shies away when his mouth nears hers.

Suddenly she wriggles from his arms, throws back the covers, maneuvers down to his erect penis, and devours it. Afterward, she swallows his semen. Then she situates herself above him, straddling his face, pushing her crotch toward his mouth. Castro, self-conscious, feels in the dark for the light switch and turns it off.

In the impassioned darkness, it sounds like a mastiff lapping from a water bowl.

Chapter 26

The truck stops in Plaza Peñarroya, and the five soldiers traveling in the back next to crates of ammunition jump out and bid the driver good day.

The driver raises a hand in bored acknowledgment and rides off.

An icy wind cuts through the air. Castro zips up his sweater and raises the lapels on his cape.

"So the good times are over, eh?" someone in line at the bakery shouts.

He recognizes Alonso, the second-company quartermaster. They shake hands.

"Yep, back again; see what happens next. How're things going?"

Alonso's nose is red and he's got chilblains on his ears. He's wearing three pairs of socks and gigantic boots. He jumps up and down, attempting to warm his blood. When he talks, a thick cloud of mist forms in front of his mouth.

"So-so. The party's over for the reds; little by little they're losing the ground they took, the towns they captured. We got more Moors and legionnaires for reinforcements. How was Burgos?"

"Well, what can I say? I stuffed myself silly, then got sent back. What can you do?"

Alonso looks both ways before asking confidentially, "So, the war's about over, right? What's the word?"

"How should I know?"

"Shit, Castro! You're up there rubbing elbows with Franco and you don't even bother to find out when this is all going to end?"

"What does he know?"

"Everything! He knows everything, you idiot. The reds are screwed, see. They already lost Asturias, and now they've lost Cataluña, and that's where the mines and industry are. But for some reason we don't have the stomach to crush them once and for all."

"Well, I'm going to get back to my company. They still on Cerro del Médico?"

"Still there."

"How hard will it be to get a ride?"

"I think there're trucks at the depot heading back."

It turns out the trucks have already left, but Castro finds Commander Medina's liaison, who's waiting for some lists to come in from headquarters.

"What'd you come back for, you fool? We got bombarded yesterday. Two dead and three wounded. Don't go thinking the war's over yet."

"Can you take me back to the front?"

"If you insist, man. But you'll have to wait 'til this afternoon; I got a bunch of paperwork and it's going to take a while."

Castro's in no rush. He thinks about Concha. Over the last few days he's had a lot of time to reflect. *We could be friends, if nothing else. When the war's over . . . something might come of it. You never know.* It's occurred to him on more than one occasion that don Federico might want to reward the sacrifice his father and family made for the nationalist cause. The Castros could have bitten the hand that fed them, the way so many did, but instead, his father went to jail, his mother and sisters went hungry, and he joined the nationalists and was decorated by Franco. Don Federico might be generous, might give his family the Calzones' plot on La Quintería and that orchard Castro's father likes so much. Castro imagines his father kissing don Federico's hand, crying, his mother wringing the ends of her apron, weeping too. "God bless you, don Federico; you're a saint and a great solace to the poor!" With Valentina and another mule he'll buy, he might be able to make some money off that little farm, then rent out land, prosper. . . . The war might benefit him after all. "As long as I've got these two hands," he pictures himself saying to Concha, "you won't want for anything; you're going to live like a queen." Besides, he's a hero now; he's been in the papers, been talked about on the radio. Concha might be regretting that fateful day.

Without realizing it, his feet have taken him to Pensión Patria. The door's shut; the shutters are closed. On the window he sees a little sign, hanging from a wire, in Concha's writing. *This business has moved to the old Engineers' House across the plaza.*

Business is clearly going well. The new "Hotel Imperial" is a fancier building, with a well-tended garden out front below the main balcony. Castro walks through the main gate. The door is half open, leading into a spacious entryway with a glass-covered display case holding a Virgin of Carmen and Child statue and scapulars and a little slot for donations. On the wall, a large photo of the Caudillo shares top billing with a color lithograph of the Virgin of Perpetual Succor, which Castro remembers from their old *pensión*. Their servant is mopping the hydraulic floor tiles, kneeling on a plank, dipping the mop into a chipped zinc bucket.

"Hi, Luisa. Is Concha here?"

The maid stands and wipes her swollen red hands on her apron. She can't hide her joy at seeing the corporal.

"*Ay,* I'm so glad to see you again, sir! You looked so

handsome in the paper! Don't tell the *señorita* I told you this, but we were all so happy here to see you in the newspaper! Miss Concha is upstairs in her room. Wait just a minute and I'll go tell her you're here."

She lifts the edge of her apron and rushes up the elegant staircase. Castro enjoys watching her generous bottom until it disappears from sight as she turns on the landing. He runs his hands through his hair, smooths his new army jacket, and adopts what he considers an interesting pose, so that when she comes down, Concha will see him admiring the paintings, which might be originals belonging to the mining engineers who owned the house: four Greek or Roman domestic scenes of women in tunics, black slaves, smoking censers, columns, murals, and nymphs. In one painting, one of the women's breasts are exposed, but the new owners have scratched them out so as not to offend their guests' sense of decency.

"Hello, Juan."

Castro turns. Concha is standing at the top of the stairs, elegant and erect, smiling and beautiful, in her patterned robe; the maid is standing behind her, sobbing uncontrollably.

"Have Luisa take you into the sitting room. I'll be right down."

Concha takes over half an hour to reappear. When she does, she's radiant, wearing a round-necked polka-dotted dress Castro's never seen before, accentuated by a silver bracelet; she's teased her bangs and applied soft red lipstick. She closes the door and sits beside Castro at one end of the sofa, looking prettier than ever.

"Well, you certainly made yourself scarce," she says in friendly reproach.

As if she didn't remember the last time they met!

"Well, Concha, after what happened . . . Look, I came because I can't stop thinking about you."

Moved, Concha's chest heaves with a deep sigh. Her eyes brim with tears. She reaches out a hand and places her cold fingers on the corporal's lips. "Please, don't say a word. You have no idea how I've suffered."

She looks down at her hands, playing with a silver ring. Then, in a broken voice, she murmurs, "I didn't realize how much I loved you. . . . The day the reds attacked, suddenly I thought I'd lost you. . . . It's been torture, with no news from you! These past few days . . ."

He inches closer and takes her hand. He hesitates, doesn't know whether or not to hug her. Concha throws herself into his arms, offers him her lips. Castro dares to kiss her and she kisses back, her lips open, her mouth round, wet, cinematic, lingual; it's a Rudolph Valentino kiss, the girlfriend yielding to the sheik's son. Castro wonders if this isn't Concha's first real kiss.

"Juan, you don't need to lie to win me over. You don't need Lieutenant Estrella's help. I just want you."

Upon hearing the name, he recalls one of Lieutenant

Estrella's observations: "Women are born knowing many things that men have to learn."

Two hours fly by, two hours of kissing, touching, promises of eternal love. She makes Castro tell her every detail about his trip to Burgos, especially the open-air Mass and Franco's decoration. Needless to say, he neglects to mention Pilar.

When they say good-bye, Castro feels he's never been so happy in his life. Life is full of joy, and suddenly that ugly mining town, made even uglier by war, is the most beautiful place on earth. It's like a movie: He's traveled, the Caudillo gave him a medal, he got his girl back, it's all just been one good turn after another, and there's surely more to come. It turns out the war, which is almost over anyway, has brought him a run of good fortune: He hasn't been injured, hasn't killed anybody, met Concha, and is on the victors' side, with a medal from Franco.

He returns to headquarters. Commander Medina's liaison is finishing up with the official paymaster general. They'll be done in half an hour.

Castro slips into the noncommissioned officers' bathroom, closes the door, and masturbates, fantasizing about Concha. She let him get further than ever today; he even touched her nipples.

Chapter 27

The mules are grazing, hobbled in the pasture, facing away from the stables. Castro approaches Valentina. He strokes her and lets her sniff him. She inhales several times before recognizing the corporal's scent. He's too clean. Then she nuzzles up against him in welcome.

Heliodoro comes out to urinate and sees him.

"What the— Castro, shit, you back already, you fool?"

"In the flesh, man. I missed you guys."

The muleteers come out to give him a hug. He passes out the five bottles of cognac he's got in his knapsack, one of which was a gift from Pilar; the others he bought in train stations on the way back.

Inside the farmhouse they've got a good stick fire going. They made *migas* and there's still some left in the pan. As he eats, Castro answers his comrades' questions.

"What's Franco like?"

"Franco's ... small. Not tall, that's for sure, and he's got a little potbelly, so when he walks it looks like the tassels on his sash hang straight down to the ground. His feet are really small, too, even inside his tall boots and spurs, and"—he hesitates—"well, he has sort of a big ass." He glances at his fellow soldiers and then, in an attempt to mitigate the effect of this last comment, quickly adds, "He's got presence, that's for sure. Very commanding, all he has to do is raise an eyebrow or cock his head and all the generals are scared shitless, like he was God! But the funniest thing is his voice. It's not all big and booming—no, sir. He's got a kind of quivery, shrill voice that's ... well, delicate."

"You mean he *spoke* to you?" Heliodoro asks.

"Well, I mean, he didn't actually speak to *me,* no. We walked up and he pinned the medals on us. They'd already told us to fold a pleat into our army jackets, 'cause all they do is stick the pin part through it, and then once you're back in your seat, you fasten it yourself so it doesn't get lost."

Petardo examines the medal, front and back.

"Hey, are you supposed to wear this all the time?"

"Oh sure, all I need is for some commie sniper to set his sights on me, think I'm an officer, and take me out!

No way, man, this little guy's going back in his case and, when the war's over, into the china cupboard."

Castro's house, of course, has no china cupboard, but he's seen them in dining rooms before and in the Los Escoriales hunting-trophy room, which is full of trays and assorted curios. With all the money he's earned, he'll pay the carpenter to make him a display cabinet for the medal.

"Bet you got laid," Pino says.

"Course he did!" Heliodoro replies. "Don't even have to ask." And he looks at Castro expectantly, awaiting confirmation.

"Come on! Tell us..."

The circle of attentive faces leans in.

Castro sighs and clucks his tongue.

"Well, what can I say? After the ceremony that night, we were in the barracks back at headquarters, after dinner.... You know what they gave us for dinner?"

"What?"

"They gave us this stew from León that you eat backward. You start with the meat: pork, beef, lamb, chorizo, blood sausage, and bacon."

"Man, you're making my mouth water!" Heliodoro says. "Was there a lot of it?"

"A pot for every six. We stuffed ourselves. And that was just the first course; after that came garbanzos—really tiny ones, delicious—and last, the broth for whoever wanted it, to perk you up."

"Great, fantastic. Tell us about the whores," Pino says, deadpan.

"Okay, okay. Well, what do you expect? There we were, no guards, no rules, it was like a hotel, you could come and go as you please, you know? So the legionnaire says, 'Hey, why don't we go celebrate, pick up some hookers?' So we went and found this classy place, Fenómena's.

"So we're going back and forth trying to decide if it's worth the money—'cause this place was *expensive*—when the pilot says, 'Fuck it, you only live once; we might be dead tomorrow!' So we went in and, man, you wouldn't believe it! Real classy. The curtains, the furniture, the mirrors... there was even a piano! And Fenómena comes out wearing this dress that looks like a curtain, and she's got huge tits, and she starts fawning all over us: '*Ay*, what an honor, the heroes of the fatherland!' Can you believe it? The lady recognized us!"

"She *recognized* you?"

"That's what I said! Seems she was one of the ladies wearing a *mantilla* at the Mass when Franco gave us the medals!"

"But... wasn't she a hooker?"

"Not a hooker, a *madam*," Pino interrupts. "Fancy hookers have madams, and they rub elbows with everybody, even bishops."

The others stare in disbelief.

"Anyway," Castro continues, "she called down the girls, just like at Misangre's place but nicer, and I set my eye on this little blonde named Pilarín, and we went up to the room in an elevator."

"In an *elevator*?"

"An elevator. I'm telling you, they had everything in that house. An iron elevator, really fancy. Anyway, so we go up to the next floor and she takes me to a room, the fanciest room you've ever seen, with a bed like a hayrick, big and soft, with two wool blankets and a bunch of big soft pillows, everything smelling like lavender and quince. And would you fucking believe the girl goes and locks us in and says, 'Now we're going to take a bath.' And then she gives me a bath, like a little kid."

"In a washbasin?" Heliodoro wants to know.

"Forget washbasins, man! In an iron tub bigger than three troughs put together! The water was hot, steamy, and she put in some powder that smelled like cologne. It was unbelievable. And once I was all clean, she tells me to get out and dries me off with a towel as big as a sheet."

"Oh, come on!" Petardo whines.

"I'm telling you, it was big as a sheet!"

"Would you get to the good stuff!" Pino complains. "Then what?"

"Then we went to bed. A big four-poster bed, really tall. Anyway, after that banquet, my dick was about to explode. So I go to touch her—man, you wouldn't believe the tits she had! As soon as I grabbed them, her nipples went like chestnuts, big and hard. And then..."

Castro pauses for dramatic effect. His friends sit enraptured, and nothing they've ever heard will compare to what Castro is about to say.

"She pushes me back and puts my dick in her mouth."

"She put your dick in her *mouth*?"

Castro nods solemnly.

"Shit!"

"Just like that?" Pino asks, incredulous. "You didn't even ask?"

"Didn't even ask," Castro confirms.

"Fuck, man! That's class!" Heliodoro exclaims.

"Anyway, so when I came, she sucked my dick like it was a can of condensed milk, didn't leave a single drop. Then she went into the bathroom, which was right in the room, behind a screen, and I heard her spit and gargle, but me, I was in seventh heaven."

"Jesus!" Pino says. "You're so lucky!"

"Best twenty-five *pesetas* I ever spent in my life."

"I think we're all going to have to jack off tonight," Aguado concludes.

"Well, every dog licks his own balls," Petardo says.

They each go back to their business. Castro lights a cigarette and remains pensive, sitting on the broken trough. By depicting Pilar as a whore—instead of the wealthy, willing woman of class she is—Castro somehow feels he hasn't disrespected the memory of their encounter. He goes out to see Valentina. He pats the top of her neck and scratches the underside. Valentina presses her giant head against his chest, and he runs a finger across her sleep-encrusted eyelid.

"How you doing, Valentina? Did Chato treat you all right? Bet you thought I wasn't coming back, eh?"

The mule looks at Castro with her huge eyes, waggles her head, and rubs up against him. He pets her, scratches behind her ears.

"*Ay*, Valentina, if only you knew!"

He thinks about Pilar and her earth-shattering orgasms, the way she screamed in pleasure, her lack of concern about the neighbors hearing...

"If you knew what the world was like out there..."

He thinks about Burgos, about Franco, about the trains, the towns, all the things he's seen.

"Know what I think? I just want all this shit to be over, the war to end, and us to go back to La Quintería. It's only three days from here, with good grass. I'll grab my pack, get some bread, a few onions from the quartermaster, fill a canteen with wine, and we'll head off to La Quintería. We've got no business here. Just you wait and see how they react when I turn up with a new mule and more than four hundred *pesetas*. My mother'll cry; I can just picture her, drying her hands on her apron. 'My boy's back, *ay*, Holy Virgin of Perpetual Succor, you brought him back alive!' My father'll thump his shepherd's hook on the ground, pretending he's not excited. He'll have been released from prison after the red lines break. And my sisters, when they scream it'll be louder than the reds bombarding! Don't let it scare you, though."

The mule sniffs her master, nostrils flared.

"I still don't stink enough for you, eh, Valentina?" Castro laughs. "Well, don't worry, we'll take care of that soon enough. Just give me a week and I'll be full of lice and smell like shit."

Chapter 28

February 3, 1939. Fourth Triumphal Year. The Twenty-second Division of the Guadalquivir Army Corps leaves the trenches on Cerro del Médico and Mano de Hierro, advancing their positions to the crest of Cerro de la Antigua after the Marxist advance was lost on January 5.

The red army, hungry and demoralized, puts up little resistance. Beneath a dreary rain, along a muddy trail, the Second Transport Battalion mule train advances with a load of machine guns, stretchers, ammunition, saucepans, and other utensils for the camp kitchen. From over toward Cerro Rasero comes the din of intermittent shelling.

Castro's opted for the road that skirts Gamonal, running parallel to the Pozo stream, so the convoy will be hidden by all the dwarf oaks and holm oaks if any red planes fly over. He's at the front, followed by Chato and the others, and Pino is last. Each driver has three mules in his train. For some time now, they've been watching a column of smoke rise up from behind the hills.

"Bet they set fire to the Cruz *cortijo*," Pino guesses.

"Doubt it," Aguado replies. "Black smoke comes from gasoline and tires. That's got to be a truck. But if it broke down and they couldn't fix it, they probably just set it on fire so we couldn't requisition it."

When they get over the hill they see the source of the smoke down below: a T-26 tank in flames, flipped over in a ditch. As they get closer, they find several bodies strewn among the shrubs in the field. They pick their way along in silence, avoiding the corpses. Many lie faceup, their arms spread, glassy eyes staring up at the sky, mouths open— which means that some Moors (and some Spaniards) have already been through, looking for gold teeth. Some of the bodies have their ring fingers cut off.

As they pass the tank, Castro gets a sick feeling.

"Wait here a minute," he orders his men.

He ties Valentina to a tree and goes over to examine the dead. Three partially charred bodies lie beside the tank. They're wearing grease-stained blue boilersuits and leather jackets. Soviet tank helmets cover their heads. And they're barefoot, having been robbed of their boots. One body, taller than the rest, lies facedown.

Castro approaches and, after a moment's hesitation,

leans down and flips him over. It's Churri, his bony face black with grease and smoke. His glassy eyes are half open, and he's got the distinctive beaklike nose that corpses always seem to have. His mouth is relaxed, almost smiling.

Castro feels like he's been punched in the stomach; then the sensation rises to his throat and he can't breathe. He falls to his knees in the mud, his eyes blurry, tears streaming down his cheeks.

"Churri!" He hugs the corpse, presses it to his chest and cradles it. "Churri!" he whispers, his voice distorted, un-recognizable. "How could you go and die now, when the war's almost over? We were going to have such good times back in La Quintería. *Ay,* Churri, what a waste. What good is everything we've done now, everything we've seen? . . . Who'm I going to run around with now? What about all those things you were going to teach me?"

Corporal Castro cries silently, hugging the militiaman's body, rocking it like a mother would a sleeping baby. The other drivers are standing around awkwardly, waiting some distance off, looking at one another, somber, silent, not knowing how to react.

"He was from the same town," Chato explains. "They were close."

"Fuck. Well, looks like he won't be giving anyone any more trouble," Heliodoro observes.

Chato shoots him a furious glance.

"You mind shutting the fuck up?"

Aguado hands Petardo his mules' lead rope and walks over to Castro.

"Juan, there's nothing you can do for him now, and the guys in the company need weapons and ammo."

Castro nods. He wipes his tears and snot on his army-jacket sleeve. Then slowly, gently, he places Churri's body back down on the ground and wipes a blade of grass from his face.

"I want to give him a proper burial; I don't want the dogs getting to him."

"Fuck, Juan, we have to deliver this ammo!" Aguado insists. "We'll come back and bury him later."

Castro returns to the group, head bowed, and unfetters Valentina. He sighs deeply.

"Come on, then. Let's go!"

They continue along the trail, heading north in silence. Castro drapes the lead rope around his neck and under his arms, like the harvesters back home, and walks with his hands in his pockets, his head down. Going up the little hill, they pass the Antigua chapel. He crosses himself furtively and says a silent Our Father for his friend who didn't believe in God. Maybe Churri was right, like he was about so many other things. But at times like this, you really hope there's someone waiting on the other side.

They reach the new lines at Fuente la Zarza *cortijo*, by Cerro de Los Pedroches, where the second company is digging ditches for marksmen in the wet ground. Sharpshooters can be heard in the distance, and once in a while there's cannon fire too. At the command post there are half a dozen spindly, high-axle Russian trucks they've seized from the reds, their headlights protected by a little metal grille in an iron semicircle. There are a couple of ambulances, too, with enormous red crosses on the roofs and doors. Castro convinces the quartermaster to lend him a motorcycle and sidecar. Heliodoro knows how to drive it. With Chato on the back and himself squeezed into the narrow sidecar, the three of them return to the ditch where Churri lies beside the smoking tank. His body looks the same as it did when they left it; if anything, his lips are a little paler beneath a thin film of grease. Castro points to the foot of a leafy holm oak.

"There."

They grab the pick and shovel and take turns digging until they've made a ditch almost three feet deep. Castro searches the body: nothing. His pockets have been emptied. A few feet away, Heliodoro finds a ripped oilskin wallet, empty, with two ID cards, one from the Iberian Anarchist Federation and the other, the republican army: *Benito Alcántara Expósito, Lieutenant in the Republican People's Army, 47th Division, tank platoon.* Castro takes the wallet and puts it with the partially blown-apart dog tags Churri had around his neck.

The corpse's arms are outstretched. He's completely stiff, so they have to struggle to force the awkward body into the ditch. They shovel dirt back in until the grave is covered, piling what's left of the upturned earth into a little hill that Castro tops with a few large rocks.

"A grave marker."

He's decided to go to Churri's house to tell his mother and sisters that he buried him with his own hands. Maybe they'll think he killed him. They were on opposite sides, after all. How could they understand that they'd fallen out and didn't speak to each other for years, then became friends in the middle of a war?

But that's the kind of thing that happens in wartime. People in the trenches know that, but in the rear guard there are certain things people just don't understand.

"Let them think what they want. I'll be a better friend to him after his death than when he was alive."

They return to the Pozo *cortijo* at nightfall. The first thing Castro does is go to the command post. Escámez and two other liaisons are listening to the radio.

"Quiet, quiet, they're talking about us!"

Castro perks up.

". . . troops of the Glorious National Army have broken red lines, and the Marxist troops are beating a retreat, leaving behind munitions and military supplies, trucks and other vehicles. In a month of operations in the Valle de Los Pedroches sector, the red army has suffered six thousand five hundred twenty-six casualties, which our forces have buried. The Glorious National Army has taken six thousand four hundred eighty-four prisoners, captured twelve tanks, rendered thirty-two others useless, and commandeered over two hundred machine guns and four thousand rifles. Marxist casualties are estimated at over forty thousand. In Cataluña, a ship belonging to the red armada..."

"Hey, Escámez, give me the report, I've got work to do."

The clerk opens a rubber notebook and hands the muleteer a form.

Castro records the date and the number of mules—same as always—twenty-four, and five horses. As always, where it says *Incidents* he writes *None* and then signs below. He hands the form back to Escámez, who places it in the notebook.

"Bye."

No one replies. They're hanging on the radio reporter's every word.

It's cold, and the humidity hurts Castro's lungs. There's frost on the ground. He turns toward the nearby lights and sees a fire burning behind one of the farmyard walls, where the quartermaster has set up his stores.

"Cacho, you know where my men are?"

The battalion muleteers are inside a shed on the other side of the grounds. He walks over to the mules and hears Chato singing quietly.

While you're in bed asleep
I'm down here on the street

Your tits are nice and hot
My dick's hard as a rock

Castro laughs.

"The war's over, Valentina! We're going home. I wish poor Churri could come, too. . . ."

Chato saved some dinner for him. While he inhales his cold meat stew with white beans and garbanzos, Castro thinks about the *migas* he and Churri had one day at Los Escoriales back in the fall of 1934, in the ruins of a Roman mine, while they made plans for the future. They were going to get engaged at the next Feria de Sevilla, both of them, to the two prettiest girls in town. Of course, things didn't quite turn out like they'd planned. *Things never turn out how you want them to,* Castro thinks glumly. *If it's not one thing it's another. At least for poor people.*

A noisy downpour falls on the corrugated asbestos roof. In the shed, behind the stables, the muleteers have dug a drainage channel in case it floods. There's enough space left to spread blankets out on the hay. Castro counts the lumps beneath the blankets, all lined up. If they weren't all snuggled up in the fetal position, they'd look like a row of corpses awaiting burial. Heliodoro and Petardo are snoring. Aguado and Amor, unable to sleep, are talking in hushed tones. Aguado thinks they started off the war as thrifty as possible, never firing a shot if they didn't need to, and now here they are with it almost over and they're going to have leftovers of everything.

"You've seen all those planes, they're coming nonstop, bombing left and right. Yesterday I heard one of our guys shot up the Twenty-third. No one snuffed it, but a few guys got really fucked up."

"Great. Just when we're about to be discharged, they come and fuck with their own side!"

"Exactly."

Amor elbows his companion and nods toward the door. Aguado turns and sees Castro making up his bed.

"We'll all just have to wait and see what things are like at home, when we get there."

Then they keep silent until they fall asleep. After the downpour, the sky clears and the moon periodically peeks out—round, enormous, partially covered by wispy black clouds. In the eerie moonlight, the mules' wet backs glisten.

On March 26, 1939, at dawn, the four corps of the nationalist Army of the South effortlessly advance on the wide front between the Zújar River and the Guadalquivir, unaccompanied by the thunder of mass artillery fire, just a few reconnaissance planes flying overhead. The reds come out of their trenches and fall back with no resistance. Two columns advance on Puertollano and Ciudad Real without firing a shot, and a third one advances on Pozoblanco. Entire battalions surrender, waving the white flag. The official report from Burgos announces the total collapse of the front. The Fortieth Division reaches Minas de las Morras de Cuzna; the One hundred second Division crosses the river. On the Madrid front, red soldiers in the Bombilla zone lay down their arms and fraternize with the nationalists, singing and drinking together.

The Twenty-second Division advances toward Hinojosa del Duque with the Army of Africa.

The mid-morning sun shines clear and bright. The Canaries battalion muleteers are riding their mules, having nothing to transport, along the Valsequillo road. They come upon one of Yagüe's columns of Moors.

Hobbling along, Mohammed recognizes Castro.

"You still alive, my friend?"

"Aren't you happy to see me, Mohammed? I'm not planning on dying anytime soon."

"Where are your things, your provisions?"

"You think I carry everything with me, like you do? The supplies are up front, in the trucks."

"War over, eh?"

"Looks like it. Time to go home."

"I hear reds are giving up boats and planes too."

"Might be true; you don't see hardly any around."

"War over in Madrid too?"

"I think so. I think it's over in Madrid too."

"*Ay*, too bad. I want to go to Madrid. Lot of red women there, lot of rings, lot of sewing machines."

"What you need to be doing, Mohammed, is getting

back home to your little Moor wife, even if you have to limp all the way. You been through enough here; it's time for everybody to get on home."

"What about your earring lady? She happy?"

"Yeah, real happy," Castro lies. He's kept the earrings in his jacket pocket, wrapped in tissue paper. For some reason, he didn't return them to Concha when he last saw her. Perhaps he'll save them for Jacinta, who's all grown up.

They take their leave. Castro carries on down his path with the mule train, deep in thought as he makes his way into the oak grove.

"You know the first thing I'm going to do when we're discharged?" Heliodoro asks.

No one replies; he just continues.

"When I get home, I'm going to take two mattresses and put them in a room with no light, I'm going to lock the door, and I'm going to sleep for three days straight."

"You're not even going to eat first?"

Heliodoro considers it.

"Not even going to eat first. There's never much to eat at my house, anyway."

Cresting a steep slope, they come upon a well and, sitting in the shade of the arbor covering it, a dozen republican soldiers. They have no weapons—at least none in sight—but Castro stops the train, wary. A red sergeant sees him and wearily takes a white handkerchief from the top pocket of his army jacket, waving it listlessly.

"Hey, don't worry, friend, we come in peace; we're on

our way to surrender. Just taking a little rest. We left Villanueva de Córdoba this morning, and our feet are all messed up."

"Where're your poppers?" Castro asks.

"Our rifles? Back there. We left our belts too. Everything. The officers told us the war was over and took off in the regiment car. Probably in France by now."

Castro's not about to take any prisoners, even if they beg him on bended knee, so he says, "Well, you'll get to the command post if you take that path. It's in a farmhouse about four kilometers from here. Any of you from Andújar?"

"There was a guy from Andújar in my company."

"What happened to him?"

"Who knows. He went the other way this morning, with two other guys. He might've said he was going to Jaén. I think the fascists are in Venta de Cárdenas already."

Chapter 29

The Hotel Imperial is swarming. Now that the war's ending, refugees are returning and taking rooms while they get the homes they evacuated years ago back in order.

"Hi, Luisa. Is Concha here?"

Luisa can't mask her alarm.

She's about to respond, when Concha appears at the dining-room door. "Hello, Juan."

He sees a strain in her expression he hasn't noticed before. "How are you, Concha? Is everything all right?"

"No, not quite. Wait for me out in the plaza and I'll be right out."

With all the moving, the plaza is in a state of frenzy.

Munitions trucks, tractors towing pieces of heavy artillery, carts, and trains of horses.

Castro greets a few familiar faces. The word is that the war's going to end any time, in a few days, maybe even a few hours. Thirty minutes later Concha appears in street clothes. Before Castro can lean down to kiss her cheek, she turns away and starts walking.

"How about we take a walk?" she says, solemn.

"Sure."

They take the Villanueva road, which is slightly less frenetic.

"Do you mind telling me what's wrong?" the corporal asks.

She bursts into tears.

"Concha, what is it?" Castro's worried now. "Tell me, my love! Did you have a fight with your mother?"

She pouts, wipes her tears with a little handkerchief she pulls from her sleeve, and takes a deep breath to calm herself, avoiding Castro's eyes.

"What it is, Juan, is that it's over between us."

Castro looks at her, disconcerted. "What did I do?"

"It's not you, you didn't do anything; you're a good man. It's just that I . . . I can't see you anymore!"

"But—"

"No, don't interrupt me. Let me speak; it's hard enough as it is." Her beautiful, tearful eyes now look into his. "Listen. I've been writing you letters for days and ripping them up because I can't figure out how to say it. It's better if I just tell you straight from the heart. We love each other so much right now; everything's going well, but this can't last . . . because . . . I know it can't last . . ."

"But why?"

"It just can't."

"There must be a reason. You ought to at least tell me why, let me know."

"Because we're young now, and everything is perfect, but the war is going to end any day, and when it does, then what's going to happen?"

"What do you think? We'll get married and have children, like everybody else."

"Yes, Juan, I know. You're a good man, but what future would we have on a farm?"

"Well, if you want, we can live in town."

"What I mean is, you're a country boy, you're a mule driver, and you could never offer me another sort of life."

"What kind of life?"

"The kind I want: dresses and treats and . . . I don't know . . ."

"As long as I've got two good hands, my love, you'll never want for anything, and our children won't either! I'll do whatever I can. Besides, you're not the kind of girl who wants a life of luxury."

"Says who?" Concha snaps, irritated. "Yes, I am! It's just that you met me during wartime, with all this misery, when I couldn't have what I wanted, but I dream of a life

of comfort, the life of a lady, not out in the countryside
where you live like animals. . . ."

They walk on in silence. Castro is trying to take in what
he's just heard. Concha, who'd said that being a muleteer
was honorable, now suddenly would be comfortable only
with the gentry. Now Castro understands her unflagging
determination to try to get him to stay in the army after
the war. Once she tried to convince him that a corporal
decorated by Franco in person would soon be promoted
to sergeant and, with a little luck, could retire a lieutenant
or, who knows, even a captain. But Castro didn't want to
be sentenced to life in the barracks. It wasn't for him.

"I wasn't expecting this," Castro says bitterly, after a
few minutes.

"I know you weren't. That's why I had to tell you
straight out. You're a good man, but you have no other
means, and you're not the person I need. I want to have
children and raise them decently, not out in the country
with pigs and chickens."

"That's how I was raised."

"Precisely! And I don't want my children to be like you.
I have other aspirations."

Castro is stunned into silence.

"It's better if we don't see each other anymore. I've got
your gifts and photos and letters here." She hands him a
little packet tied with blue ribbon. "I've already returned
those dirty earrings, of course. You can send me mine

tomorrow, with your company's quartermaster or anyone who comes into town."

She holds out her hand, which Castro barely even touches.

"Good-bye, Juan."

"Don't you even want me to walk you back?"

"No, don't bother. I'd rather go back alone."

She starts off, a little wobbly on her heels. Castro wants her more than ever.

"*Ay,* Valentina! I knew I wasn't the man for her, but I tried to pretend. She wants a lieutenant and I'm a nobody, even with Franco's medal pinned on."

He retraces his steps and walks through the market, which consists of a few stands in Plaza de la Fuente. He buys two *reales'* worth of *churros* and sits on the curb, lost in thought.

"Sir!"

It's the servant from Hotel Imperial, weighed down with a huge palm basket with onion tops peeking out.

"Hello, Luisa."

She looks both ways, not wanting anyone to see them together.

"Sir, I'm so sorry, because you're a good person, but I have to tell you something, if you swear on something you truly love that you'll keep this secret."

Castro guesses it's something to do with Concha, maybe the reason for her sudden change in conduct. As if it weren't obvious.

"I swear."

"No! Not like that! Make a cross and kiss it."

Castro crosses his index finger behind his thumb and kisses it.

"I swear."

"Sir, the girl's leaving you because she's got a sergeant major from Córdoba after her; very handsome he is too. Her father inquired about him, and he's from a very good family; they run a fabric shop in Plaza de la Corredera and he's an only child. Plus, he wants to stay on in the army. I have to go now. If anyone finds out I told you, they'll fire me."

She makes as if to leave but then remembers something and rushes back.

"Oh! And you should know that Doña Concha is the one who put her up to this; she's meaner than a pack of wild dogs. She just kept saying, 'The dirtiest pig gets the best acorn.' Anyway, now I really must go, I should have been back already."

Chapter 30

April 1, 1939. Victory Year. At eleven that night, Castro is shoeing Pastora by the light of a carbide lamp in the stables of the Cruz *cortijo* when he hears horns honking. He looks outside and sees the battalion's truck zigzagging along, as if the driver were drunk. Ramírez, the third-company quartermaster, has his body halfway out the passenger window, and he's shouting, "The war's over! It's over! The reds surrendered! *¡Arriba España!* It's over! No more! We're discharged!"

The truck doesn't stop in time and flattens a young almond tree.

Commander Castillo comes out.

"What the fuck is going on?" he demands of a liaison. "What's he saying?"

"The war's over, Commander!"

Commander Castillo shoos a starving dog that's come to sniff his boots. The quartermaster jumps out of the truck and rushes to report, tears in his eyes.

"Commander, sir, the war's over!"

The news spreads. Within a minute, half the company has congregated in front of the farmhouse.

The commander interrogates the quartermaster.

"Who says so?"

"They announced it on the radio in town, an hour ago! Fernando Fernández de Córdoba read the Generalísimo's report! The war is over!"

The commander falls silent. He bangs his cane down on a pebble. He's from a town in the province of Castellón and hasn't heard from his parents in three years. He lost two brothers in the war, and he'll have to deliver the news to his mother himself.

"It's about time," he murmurs, returning to his command post to telephone headquarters.

The news spreads like wildfire through the trenches, farmhouses, barricades on the Perdiz plain, to the farthest outposts: The war is over! People shout *vivas,* toss their caps into the air, dance. *¡Viva España! ¡Viva* Franco! *Viva* the Babies' Brigade!

"And the sweet-tooth column!"

"*Viva* the sweet-tooth column!"

"*Viva* Christ the King!"

A few soldiers move away from the uproar to cry. One says to his friend, "We'll be home by harvest time."

Some remain silent. Most laugh. One fires a shot into the air and a sergeant gives him a harsh reprimand.

For days, soldiers on the other side have been wandering, scattered, in all directions. No weapons, no insignia, hungry, waving white flags they've improvised out of sheets. Division command fenced in the entire town of Valsequillo with barbed wire as a makeshift concentration camp for the thousands of prisoners and defectors until they established who was responsible for what.

Castro finishes shoeing Pastora, gives her to Chato to take back to the stables, and heads to the Pura farm. In the office, the colonel and half a dozen officers are gathered around Sergeant Sánchez's radio while he fiddles with the dial in an attempt to get rid of the static. Suddenly the announcer's voice booms clearly, "—niards! War report from the Generalísimo's headquarters: Today, with the red army captive and disarmed, nationalist troops have achieved their final objectives. The war is over. Burgos, April first, 1939. Generalísimo Francisco Franco Bahamonde."

The soldiers outside cheer. "¡*Viva España! Viva* the Third Battalion! *Viva* the Falange!"

The sergeant berates them, "Quiet, quiet! They might say something else!"

As the hissing interference grows louder, the familiar strains of the Legion's hymn begins. A sergeant major with long sideburns bursts into song: "I'm a valiant, loyal legionnaire..." and then falls silent again when no one else joins in.

Soldiers hug, dance, cry, clap each other on the back, congratulate one another. "We're alive! We lived through the war!" Some recall those who did not, both in sadness and relief.

"Where's the wine?"

"We have to celebrate!"

The lieutenant colonel orders an allotment of wine and another of "liquid courage" cognac to be passed out. After all, they won't be needing it for battle now.

Castro feels a sweet sorrow in his throat, a joy he can't express. He's going home, to hug his mother, his father, Jacinta—who'll be a woman now—and Manuela. He thinks bitterly of Churri, who'd seen Jacinta only a few months ago. He imagines arriving with Valentina in tow. "I brought you a mule, Father. We'll get hold of a plow, even if it's that old wooden one that's been rotting in the corner of the barn for years. That'll do at first. We'll see if it's a good harvest, 'cause we have to get things off the ground again."

He won't say a word about the fiancée he lost. Why bother, since they had never even met her?

Pino appears, euphoric, the hood of his cape on his head. He hands Castro a bottle of cognac and says, imitating a

Moor named Muza he knows, "My friend, my friend! Drink with me! You know how not to get shot!"

Castro laughs, grabs the bottle, and takes a swig. He feels the pleasant burn as it slides down his throat.

Out in the stables, Valentina is rooting through the trough, in case she's missed any stray grain. A happy mule who knew nothing of the war's existence has no cause to celebrate its end. Castro, nevertheless, gives her the news and pets her.

"Valentina, baby, the war's over. From now on, we'll have to work and earn a crust, but no more bullets. We're going to La Quintería, to the fresh grass by the river. You'll see."

The mule nuzzles Castro's chest.

"Valentinilla, we've made it through this mess and we're both alive." He gives her a kiss. "You'll see, we'll get by just fine on the farm. And when you're old and no good for work, you won't have to worry, we'll never sell you to the slaughterhouse, not after going through this war together. When you're old, you'll go to a good pasture in Solana, right by the Guadalquivir, and you'll have all the pecks of barley you'll need. Maybe I'll even put you in with the herd one day and take you to Las Viñas just for the ride, to hunt for milk caps."

The corporal scratches the back of her head as he envisions their arrival home.

"Just wait 'til they see me turn up with you."

He thinks about his family, about the tragedies of war. He doesn't want to consider Concha part of it, but he's plagued by her memory.

"*Ay*, Valentina! Who knows what else is in store for us."

A few prisoners are sitting on the ground, guarded by two soldiers, waiting for the truck that will take them to Valsequillo. Castro hears a voice with the unmistakable accent from Torre del Campo.

"Which one of you's from Torre del Campo?" he asks.

"Huh?"

A prisoner jumps up. "Are you from my town?"

"No, I'm from near Andújar, but I recognized your accent. I used to go to Torre del Campo when my mules were sick."

"Really? I'm Pachón, Peñica from Chozalhombro's nephew. My uncle used to treat mules."

"Oh, sure! I've been to his house in Chozalhombro with my father. Good man, your uncle. Raimundo, right? He still alive?"

"I saw him two months ago. He wasn't doing so good. Don't know how he is now."

"What about you?"

The prisoner shrugs.

"Fffft. We'll just have to see what they do with us now. I mean, it seems to me they have to let us go home, 'cause someone has to take in the wheat and the olives, right?"

"I hope you're right."

Castro walks off, but then he stops in the kitchen for a few crusts of bread and tins of sardines from the quarter-master. He retraces his steps and gives them to the man from Torre and his fellow prisoners.

"Here's something to tide you over, in case you're hungry."

"Hungry? We're starving!" He takes the food. "God bless you."

"No problem."

They shake hands and Castro goes on his way.

Chapter 31

April 4, 1939, the Third Battalion of the Canaries
Falange boards a freight train in Belmez, headed for Jaén.
It's got two locomotives, the front one festooned with na-
tionalist and Falange flags.

The station is swarming with soldiers burdened with
knapsacks, rifles, blankets, and assorted bundles of impedimenta. Sergeants shout themselves hoarse, liaisons
dash from one place to another in search of their officers.
From the platform roof hangs a banner that reads, *The
town of Belmez salutes and congratulates the Victorious
National Army. ¡Arriba España! ¡Viva Caudillo Franco!*

Castro tells Chato to load the mules and goes to see the
commander.

"What's the matter, Castro?"

"Nothing, Commander. I just came to ask a favor. . . ."

"Well?"

"Well, I heard the train is going through Andújar, and since my family is right there—in La Quintería, you know?—I wanted to see if I could get off to see them."

The commander shakes his head.

"No can do, Castro. We're the first nationalist troops to enter Jaén, and we have to go straight there, no stopping. Have you loaded water for the mules?"

"Yes, sir, Commander."

"Well, then, get back to your company. Don't you worry, once we get to Jaén I'll grant you leave to go see your family."

"Yes, sir, Commander!"

At ten o'clock in the morning, the engine driver blows the whistle three times and the train chugs to life and pulls out. Nineteen freight cars, with makeshift benches and canvas tops to transport the troops, and eight more cars of livestock. The muleteers travel with their animals in open-top cars. Since there are no seats, they've settled onto sacks of hay.

"This is going to be the john!" Heliodoro calls from the brake box.

Through a broken floorboard you can see the rails, the stony ground between the tracks, and the blackish ties, whizzing by faster and faster.

Aguado has managed to finagle two wineskins and a bottle of cognac. They're in high spirits, singing the

"*Carrasclás,*" greeting people who come out to watch the train pass. From time to time, Castro watches Valentina, nestled in between Romera and Barbera, in the middle of the freight car. He wonders if it's the first time she's been on a train, worries that she might spook.

"If it wasn't for the war, more than one of us'd never have been on a train," Castro comments.

"Aren't there any trains where you're from?"

"Sure, there's a station in Andújar. When I was a kid I'd go into town just to watch them pass. I used to love that. Sometimes I went with my father in the horse and buggy to pick up the Marquise of Pineda, 'cause she used to get sick in the car so she'd go on the Sevilla Express in a sleeper car instead. You know what a sleeper car is?"

They shake their heads.

"Well, I never saw one, but they say it's like a palace inside. A train with a bed inside for the marquise. It would stop only for her, so she could get off."

"First time I saw a train was when we took my brother to the hospital in Pastrana," Heliodoro says. "A cart wheel ran over his leg. It was so swollen that they had to cut it off. But then he died anyway, of gangrene."

They're silent for a while, passing the wineskin. They raise their hands to return the greeting of a group of peasants who stopped plowing to give the fascist salute upon seeing the train and flags.

"Yeah, that's the only good thing about the war, you get to see the world," Pino reflects.

"Me, I had no need to see it; I'd have been just fine at home, thank you, without this three-year curse," Heliodoro replies.

"Me too."

They fall silent again. The locomotive chugs on slowly through the olive groves, leaving a plume of billowing black smoke. After a while they're covered in coal dust, which blackens when they touch their faces. Bits fall into their eyes, which gives them an excuse for their tears.

Castro stares out at the abandoned countryside, olive trees with branches that are years old, fallow fields overgrown with scrub, untilled orchards, rickety animals in the areas where war took all the men away. They pass a young shepherd—still a boy—out grazing a dozen goats.

"Eh! The troops!" he shouts, raising his arm in fascist salute. "*¡Arriba España!*"

"Aren't you going to give us a goat?" Heliodoro cries.

The boy looks alarmed. He gathers his flock quickly and heads deeper into the olive grove.

"Ha!" Pino laughs. "He really thought we were going to take one! Do we look that bad?"

"Yeah, we do."

The train stops a couple of times due to false alarms about petards on the tracks. Rumors of Marxist guerrillas swell, reds unwilling to surrender and own up to their crimes.

It's after twelve when the train pulls into the station in

Jaén. The new provisional town council, replacing the republican one, has been awaiting the liberating troops for hours: seven councilmen and the mayor at the front, all in blue shirts. The mayor's also wearing shiny leggings.

A makeshift band welcomes the liberators with the strident opening bars of the Legion's hymn. A hundred or so school-age children wave little nationalist and Falange flags. All along the station's facade hang sheets reading, *¡Arriba España! Jaén is with the National Movement! Franco, Franco, Franco! Praise Be to the Glorious National Army!*

When the train stops, the band launches into the national anthem, which they've been practicing for days in the town-hall garage. As the troops disembark and sergeants order them to fall in, they try their hand at the *"Cara al Sol,"* which comes out as less than satisfactory.

Like all good artillerymen, the lieutenant colonel in charge is rather deaf. He tries to make himself heard by shouting at the mayor. Finally he orders, "If you don't tell your musicians to shut up, I'll have them shot!"

The mayor stands at attention, raises his arm in the fascist salute, and then scurries over to the band, his strides ungainly due to the boots, which seem too large for his feet.

"That's it! Not another note! Can't you see we're talking?"

The bandleader silences his musicians and then shrugs. "All that practice for nothing."

The photographer hired to document the event is setting up his camera on the platform. The lieutenant colonel, provisional mayor, officers, and councilmen pose before the flag-festooned locomotive. A young Falangist in the early days of her fervor, anxious to impress and to appear in the papers, loses her footing and comes crashing down onto the tracks, fat and doughy in her blue shirt and black skirt.

"Get that woman up, now!" the colonel orders. "Are you hurt, miss?"

"No, no, I'm fine," replies the injured party, adjusting her belt with a crooked smile. "*Viva* the fascist redeemers!" she cries, raising her arm from down in the train ditch.

Three or four soldiers hop down onto the tracks to make a united effort at returning her to the platform, struggling to push her up by her voluminous buttocks.

"Watch your hands!" she scolds amid the bedlam.

Castro, meanwhile, is unloading the officers' horses and the mules. Aguado has gone off to explore the station and found an abandoned storeroom.

"Quick, before anyone else gets in; we don't know how long we have to stay here!"

"But we *are* going out to find girls, right?" Pino inquires.

"We'll see."

The second and fifth companies, which are better

equipped, march to the cathedral plaza, where the councilmen will symbolically hand over the city to the liberating troops. The official ceremony has been postponed
until General Queipo de Llano himself can come to take
possession of the plaza.

The first company bivouacs close to the station. The
muleteers pile up straw to make one long makeshift mattress in the warmest part of the storehouse, which has no
windows. They spend the night taking turns huddling
around a bonfire, swigging wine and strumming a guitar.
Orphans searching for coal on the tracks come and beg
for scraps. Castro is about to give them a can of condensed milk he swiped from the quartermaster's, but little
Jacinta likes it so much that he resists the temptation, instead passing out a basket of carob beans and one *peseta*
per head, so they can buy fry cakes and chocolate.

The next day the train resumes its course, heading for
Jódar. The countryside is full of olive groves, bridges,
rivers, fallow fields, peasants who remove their caps and
give the fascist salute, standing at attention when they
catch sight of the victorious flags on the train.

"You can't fake it!" shouts a lunatic from the train. "We
know you're all reds, and we'll give you your comeup-
pance!"

A sergeant orders him to be quiet.

"Treat the civilians with respect, idiot; you have no idea
what they've been through."

At lunchtime, the train pulls into Jódar. The locomotive, now hauling only three cars, brakes too late, passes the platform, and then has to back up. The cafeteria wall has recently been whitewashed to cover the sign reading *General Union Workers for victory!* but it's still legible. A local policeman wearing a blue shirt—which is really a boilersuit with the bottoms cut off—is using railway grease to finish covering it up and rushes off on his bicycle to inform the provisional mayor that the nationalist troops have arrived.

The officers jump off. The sergeants organize the troops' debriefing. The muleteers lay ramps to unload the animals, officers' horses first.

"Thank God there's no music!" the lieutenant colonel says.

He leans on his cane like a shepherd, looking decidedly unmilitary, and contemplates the scenery: It's a large town with a castle and church supporting two tall steeples. The Sierra del Agua rises up behind it, gray and austere.

"One of my wife's uncles used to be a doctor here," a captain tells him.

"Jódar: Some name they gave this little town," another says. *Jódar* sounds remarkably like *joder,* which means *fuck.* "I don't know if we're going to allow names like that in the New Spain."

"They'll just change it, that's all," the lieutenant colonel agrees.

Castro heads out with a squad to find a house with good stables and straw to requisition. Behind the station they find a half dozen old men pounding esparto. Upon seeing the soldiers approach, they rush to stand at attention, remove their caps humbly, and give the fascist salute.

"*¡Arriba España!*" says one.

The rest echo the cheer unenthusiastically. You could tell this was new to them.

"Pardon me, sir, which way is the main plaza?" Castro asks.

"Just keep going down there, can't miss it." The old man points.

The soldiers head back up a street flanked with dusty, brittle-looking trees. A sick, rickety greyhound hangs from the branches of an old oak.

Castro is overcome by a sadness that he can't comprehend. He should be happy. The war is over, he's safe, and he'll be back with his family soon. What reason is there to be sad? Maybe contemplating the defeat, all that misery and humiliation, spoils the victory. Ever since they entered defeated Spain, he's felt plagued by the memory of Churri. Maybe he was right. The hunted beaver…

The muleteers spend that night in a big house that used to be a hospital, with good stables and graffiti on the walls. In the main room lay several beds with wool mattresses. They settle in, three to a bed. Petardo sleeps alone on a tiny mattress in the nurses' room.

"It smells like pussy in here," Pino notes on entering. "What I wouldn't have given to be here a week ago, when there were still girls around!"

"And what would you have done?" Aguado asks.

"Whisper sweet nothings...all night long, just whisper sweet nothings."

Aguado goes out to take a walk and returns with three bottles of local wine: Torreperogil red. Castro fries up some *migas,* which they eat with a few rashers of bacon. After talking late into the night, they finally go to bed, laughing uproariously because they short-sheeted Petardo's bed.

The next day the third company's first platoon climbs into two trucks and heads off to liberate Cabra de Santo Cristo, a town up in the mountains.

"Us too? But what about the mules?"

"Aren't you part of the first platoon?" Sergeant Sánchez replies. "You too. The mules stay here; the second platoon will take care of them."

Castro, Aguado, and Petardo climb in with the rest.

"But, Lieutenant, we don't even have rifles," Castro objects.

"What the fuck do you want rifles for, Corporal? Haven't you heard the war's over?"

The trucks head out, taking the mountain road, which is full of dangerous curves, potholes, and bumps. Castro is nervous: Now that the war's over, he'd rather not be separated from Valentina.

Two days later they return to Jódar.

"Nothing to report, Corporal," Chato says gravely.

"Twenty-four mules and five horses on the report," and he winks at Castro.

The commander's liaison arrives.

"Castro, get the mules ready, you're heading out to Linares tomorrow."

"Who's going?"

"First platoon. And there aren't enough trucks for everyone, so you're on foot with the mules."

At dawn they head out, taking the road to Loma and crossing the iron bridge over the Guadalquivir River.

Castro's riding Captain Arquillo's horse.

"You know what I heard?"

"What?"

"That they're going to discharge us in Linares!"

"I wish; you wait and see whether they do."

They pass the outskirts of Baeza, with fields full of grass where two scrawny goats graze, watched over by a young boy.

"*¡Viva España!*" he shouts to the soldiers, arm held high. "Got any bread?"

A soldier takes half a crust from his knapsack and tosses it down. Thinking it's a stone, the goatherd ducks, hands protecting his head. When he sees it's food, he kisses it and shouts, "Thank you, thank you! *¡Viva España! Viva* God! *Viva* the Virgin!"

In Linares, all the muleteers do is wander the streets. The livestock spend the day in the stables of some people who used to breed racehorses.

Castro writes his family a letter. He puts the most important thing at the end. *Tell Cousin Pedro to come see me however he can. It's very important.*

Castro has a plan. When Pedro gets there, he'll take the animals out to graze and give him Valentina, telling him to take her back via the main road, which goes through Villagordo and Mengíbar. And he'll finagle a sack of flour and a quarter pound of bacon from the quartermaster. He fingers his knapsack. Jacinta's condensed milk is still there.

Chapter 32

Far from the trenches, Sergeant Casimiro Pérez Aguilar didn't fire a single shot during the war, hidden away as he was in the headquarters of General Queipo de Llano's Offices of Intervention, in Sevilla. He does, however, sport the stripes he's "earned" as one of the war-wounded, having broken a leg during active duty when he slipped on a step in the air-raid shelter during an alarm.

Sergeant Pérez Aguilar, assigned to the offices of the Third Battalion of the Canaries, reports to the command post, located on Paseo del la Fuente del Pisar, in Linares. The sergeant is a meticulous man, strict and detail-oriented. Since arriving at the front two days after the war ended, he's arrested five soldiers for not saluting enthusi-astically enough, for wearing soiled uniforms, for carrying dirty armaments.

"Do you want to work?" Commander Soler asks him.

The sergeant stands firm, failing to notice the faintly facetious twitch of Soler's lips.

"I certainly do, Commander!"

"Well then, take a complete inventory of the battalion's provisions. I'm not sure if you're aware of this, but we've just been through a fucking war, three years in the thick of it, and we haven't had time to clean house."

"Yes, sir, Commander!"

The sergeant has obtained an Underwood typewriter, requisitioned from the town hall, and a thousand sheets of letter-size paper, which had once been legal-size sheets that bore the letterhead *Red Aid, Provincial Delegation of Jaén.* That part has now been cut off.

"That's what we need to do with anything that stinks of reds: Cut it off," Sergeant Pérez Aguilar quips.

The noncommissioned officer gets going on his proj-ect, aided by two assistant corporals with Military Offices insignia—bespectacled members of a champagne unit.

The regiment's record-keeping is a disaster. Every-where, things are missing: blankets, boots, caps, cartridge pouches, belts, even a 15mm mortar that, after prolonged investigation, turns out to have been left behind, forgot-ten in the Belmez train station bathroom because someone confused it with the drainpipe coming down from the roof.

The only extra thing Sergeant Pérez Aguilar actually finds is a mule. According to the battalion's reports, the regiment has twenty-four mules and five horses, but in the stable there are twenty-five mules.

"Right. Call the corporal muleteer, I want him to report," the sergeant orders.

Castro is called in. "Yes, Sergeant!"

"Are you the one who fills out the daily report for mules and horses?"

"Yes, Sergeant."

"Idiot! Can't you count? Every single report says twenty-four mules, and you've got twenty-five here!"

The sergeant corrects the report, curses Castro, and notes twenty-five in his inventory.

Castro realizes he won't be able to take Valentina home now. He's just lost the only reason for fighting his own personal war.

He walks out and sits on a stone ledge in the patio.

"Castro, cheer up, man, the mainlanders are being discharged!" Heliodoro says.

"What?" he asks distractedly.

"Anyone from the mainland is being discharged. The Canary Islanders are going home within a week, but we get to go home tomorrow. You better get down to the quartermaster's to turn in your things!"

Castro crosses the patio and walks into the stables. He approaches Valentina, scratches her neck, and lets her rub up against his army jacket.

"Valentinilla, turns out I can't take you with me; you're going to go to the Canary Islands with the regiment." He can't hold back his tears. "Well, better for you that way, Valentinilla. I have a feeling the only thing we'd have to look forward to in La Quintería is hard work, sunup to sundown, because don Federico'll return full of himself and he'll want to take it all out on the poor folks, make us pay for everything he lost in the war, so at least you'll be free of that. Besides, you'll be by the sea in the Canaries, Valentinilla: water so big you can't even see where it ends. At least you'll have that, 'cause me, I've been through this whole war, I've seen a lot of things, but never the sea."

Juan Eslava Galán was born in Andalusia, Spain, in 1948. He is the author of more than fifty books, and winner of the Planeta Award for *En busca del unicornio*. He lives in Seville.

Lisa Dillman is co-editor (with Peter Bush) of *Spain: A Literary Traveler's Companion*. She translates from the Spanish and Catalan, and teaches in the Department of Spanish and Portuguese at Emory University. She lives in Decatur, Georgia.